MONOPOLY OF GRIEF

OLUWATOYIN OMITOGUN

MONOPOLY OF GRIEF

WRITTEN BY
OLUWATOYIN OMITOGUN
tomitogun@gmail.com

Published by:
COMMUNE WRITERS INT'L
www.communewriters.com
+234 8139 260 389

Published in the Federal Republic of Nigeria

TABLE OF CONTENTS

DEDICATION

To Kemi Popoola, Femi Omitogun and Olanrewaju Omitogun; my siblings. I cherish you always.

To Oluwatobi Omitogun; my son who appeared later.

Also, to IBADAN; whose warmth and care I continue to enjoy.

I love you all.

MONOPOLY OF GRIEF

I met Laraba several years ago at Iseyin during the compulsory National Youth Service Corps orientation programme.

It was a pleasant ride from Abeokuta, through Ibadan, as I listened to the stories of travellers from different locations. From the deplorable state of the road to the threats to life, everyone was happy to have finally arrived at the camp. After securing a pass and name tag upon checking in, the next point of call was the store.

At the store, I was given two pairs of gear, one pair of socks and a small-size vest which I wanted to change. Every attempt to do so fell on deaf ears as the Officer-In-Charge merely shrugged and beckoned to the next guy on the line. I grumbled and moved on miffed at the indifference of the officer who has moved on to the next victim with his 'I care less' attitude.

'Sanjay, my man! Iseyin on the motion! A better life has come!' A voice hailed that sunny day.

My face lit up with a smile as I knew that the voice can only belong to a friend. I looked to confirm who it was.

'Ogbuefi Nnamdi!, the colonial master himself', I hailed the short stud who was already embracing me. He gave me his trademark teddy bear hug and lifted me off the floor as was his usual practice.

'This town is on fire already. How are you, my brother? Figure eight-shaped girls, booze; all have been sentenced to your territory, right?'

He asked as we moved from the entrance of the store.

'Oh boy! I am behind you o. I salute! I am fine. I just got in and trying to settle down. I have been allocated a room and I came here to collect my kit.'

I explained this to Nnamdi who was my friend's roommate at the university. I was always in their room as Kenneth and I were like two sides of a coin. Ken was posted to Cross River state and I, to Oyo State with Iseyin being the location of the orientation camp. The camp was going to be home with guys like Nnamdi for the next three weeks.

'Guy, I want to return this kit, it doesn't fit me at all. I thought it could be managed but, no way'.

'I wish you, luck brother. Let me have your hall details so we can hook up for drinks later in the day. The man in there has got a lot of attitudes and I am not ready for any ego tripping. I have resigned to my wardrobe as an alternative'.

We exchanged room details as we parted. Just then, I saw a beautiful lady of an average height, struggling with her bags, and I moved toward her. She was pretty, though on the plump side, and her face was well sculptured.

'Let me help you with this if you don't mind.'

I glanced at her endowed body and quickly looked ahead before she could catch me staring.

'Thank you, I appreciate your kind gesture'.

Her voice was tiny like a baby's as she handed the biggest bag to me with a sigh.

'Welcome to Iseyin Orientation camp. I am Sanjo Ajayi but my friends call me Sanjay'.

I introduced myself to this beautiful lady and noticed how she carried herself.

'My name is Laraba Ansa. Do you like Indian movies? I mean, with Sanjay being your nickname.'

I felt a chill down my spine and my loins responded accordingly. Her sense of humour was thrilling and her name had a certain melody attached to it. I gave her a nickname; *'Labalaba'* which meant butterfly in the Yoruba language. This was because of her colourful dress sense.

Laraba was born to a father from Angas in Plateau State and a mother from Ogbomosho, a Yoruba town in the Southwest. She had spent all her life in the northern part of the country and spoke Hausa and Yoruba languages fluently. She hides her ability to speak Yoruba until she is close enough to someone.

Laraba was different. She claimed she was a born-again Christian and does not party or socialise much. This became my albatross. She invited me to the Christian Corpers Fellowship several times but I rarely attend because of the hangover from Saturday nights. When I finally attended, I was held spellbound when I saw her in the choir singing the lead vocals for *"Amazing Grace"*, as tears welled up on many faces. I was not left out as I remember with fondness, my grandmother who was a Deeper Life member.

Since then, I have never missed Sunday Services. She was gentle and soft-spoken. Her sense of decorum, politeness and cleanliness was unrivalled. Several times, she would ask what I wanted from her.

'You, all of you', I said while holding her hands. She withdrew her hands quietly without a fuss.

'Sorry, I belong to someone else; my Lord and Saviour. I have given my all to Him', she said, gazing her at feet.

'Are you born again?' She continued.

'Yes. The moment I saw you, I got born again'. I humorously pointed to the skies, requesting the heavens to testify.

'Be serious for once in your life', she said.

Throughout the three weeks of orientation camp, we stuck together. On the night of departure, I confessed that I was falling in love with her but she laughed so hard, that it almost got me angry. She never gave a reason for the laughter. Instead, she said we should enjoy the night and forget about talks. She allowed me to hold her in my arms and nothing more.

'Let us see who you are outside this camp,' was all she said as she left for her room.

As I gaze at her picture in my bedroom in Brooklyn, New York where I'm based, I remember my Laraba who was far away in Nigeria. I came to Brooklyn after losing my job at the bank. Brownsville became my home afterwards. I hated this place with a passion! Though I had been to the United States one year earlier with Laraba, we had gone to Houston, Texas and it was a great time for both of us then. We came, not for pleasure, but to see the doctors about our childless marriage.

Laraba's faith was unwavering but I was tired of attending christening ceremonies and not having a child of my own. I loved children and wanted us to have one or two. The three weeks we spent in Houston were pleasurable and fun. We were connected to a fertility clinic in Lagos that was an affiliate of the one in Houston for follow-up. New York was a place I could stay since I had friends there. Moreover, my cousin who accommodated us during the vacation had relocated to Canada.

Brownsville was populated by African Americans and the Nigerian community there was large. Kunle was my friend from secondary school. He left for the U.S. after failing the secondary school certificate exams on several attempts. Getting a visa saved his life as he had been in New York for twenty years now. He never went back to school and had been working in low-paid jobs ever since. Alcoholism and drug problems made him unable to settle down or start a family. He has a three-bedroom apartment in the projects. It was like a hostel and transit home for immigrants from Nigeria and was also a dollar spinner for my host. We were ten in the flat altogether. Two bedrooms were occupied by four people each, while I shared the third bedroom with Kunle who snore like a moving locomotive train. With no job, I became the housekeeper.

Saturday nights were usually hell for me because Kunle's Latino woman, who was more of a hooker, would drive me out of the room. She had once asked me if I was ready for a threesome. I shook my head and ran out as Kunle's crackling laughter trailed behind me. Their time in the room was usually a shouting bout of erotic and ecstatic nonsense, followed by loud heavy metal music.

After weeks without papers for a job, and living on hand-outs from Kunle and some of the few kind guys in the flat, I got some cash from Laraba who apologised for sending little because of the high exchange rate. The other eight guys in the flat were hardly around at the same time, and when they do, they are either sleeping or getting ready for work. It was more of a transit camp, those who work day shifts rested at night while those on night shifts rest during the day.

I soon devised a strategy to make money while at home. I became a personal assistant to the nine men; for free to Kunle who was my benefactor, and to the other eight guys for a little cash. I did the laundry, cooking and ran errands instead of the housekeeper who only come in once a week and do a nasty job, leaving behind a stale smell of cheap cigarettes. On one of their free days off the streets due to IHS (Inland Home Service) threats, I got Kalu and Goke, two of Kunle's tenants, talking.

'Oh boy, is there any hope in this country for people like me who have just come in? You two have been here for years and are still on the run from immigration,' I inquired.

'Brother, there is hope. This is where hope lives. Nigeria is hell and you are here in heaven. Have you not heard of gangsters in heaven? This is just temporary, nothing much. A few days from now, the hawks will be off the streets and life goes on.' Goke said while sipping a bottle of beer. He was dressed in a ripped-out round-neck shirt over a pair of sports pants.

'If you have made it here, then there is hope for you', Kalu said as he poured some beer into his glass from Goke's bottle.

'What more hope do I need after I have been able to scale through life in Libya where I was sold into slavery by my fellow countryman? Amadi, my brother, died on the high sea after working our ass off at that camp. Days and nights on the high sea were torture in the cold. We threw some people overboard after they died in transit. The refugee camp in Italy was another experience. Some of our girls ended up in hotels, sleeping with up to ten men in one night and I still made it here to the U.S. in two years. My brother, hope is a good word in my dictionary'.

He slapped me on the back as he stood up to use the toilet.

'Sanjay, the guys who sold their organs in Israel to get here still have hope. Brother, there is hope. Hope is a tonic that keeps life moving on. People at home are praying for you to send dollars. That is why you must believe in hope.' Goke continued.

I gazed at them and could not imagine that one would dare sell his organs just to raise money to escape the economic hardship in my country. Tears welled up in my eyes, I recoiled into the sofa and was not sure whether to believe these dream merchants or just give up hope. Did I make a mistake by taking this plunge to seek a better life in the U.S.? I couldn't help but wonder.

Many times, this mess of a life would want to get to me. I was an assistant manager in a bank back home with over twenty staff and a personal driver. But here I was, living with nine other men in a strange land, with little hope for the future. At least unlike me, they have hope. Apart from Kunle, we were all illegal immigrants who had overstayed our visit.

Only one other guy was not into alcohol and prostitutes like me. Everyone was married with kids back in Nigeria but the thought of returning was the least on anyone's mind except me. I spent hours on the phone chatting and having video calls with Laraba. We held prayer vigils on the phone from the small kitchen which was the only free and quiet place in the house. My beard had been left unshaven for weeks as I got more depressed. I was in "hell" while in "heaven".

Here I was, thirty-eight years old with a wife who was childless and I'm thousands of miles away to earn a living that seems elusive. The dream of a good life in America touted at home was all a mirage. I felt like killing somebody, especially those who terminated my banking career. I was better than most of them in the university. But their fathers had looted the country and they now had money to buy banks, and fire hard-working staff like me who had put all their lives into the job.

I began to recount the opportunities I had to steal and enrich myself. I felt like a fool for not seizing the opportunities at the foreign exchange desk to stack away foreign currencies like some of the other staff. Maybe I was too stupid to not have taken advantage of the loopholes I discovered. I would have made money if not for Laraba, who had counselled that I was a Christian and should not be involved in such dirty deals.

One afternoon, I took a break from my home servicing with insignificant pay. I had refused to call Laraba for three days and had ignored her chats and calls. I was hopelessly thinking of what next to do. I don't have the papers I need to get a job, talk more of a resident permit. I now know why some immigrants end up as criminals. It was a sordid life. Unemployment, homelessness, drugs, prostitution and HIV were evident in every block and housing project. Guns were in the belt of every young man and the purses of ladies had a fair share too. Life was as cheap as ten dollars. Just then, the key turned and the door opened. I turned to see who was coming in and was surprised to see Kunle at that time of the day.

'My guy, you finally made it', he said, pointing to the bottle of beer unopened before me.

I had not touched alcohol in years. I was about to give up and end up like everyone. Why would you deny yourself pleasure for a God that will not show up when you are fired? That does not reward your faithfulness with a child? And even allowed you to languish in a foreign country without a job and hope of a better tomorrow?

'Hi, Kunle'.

I felt ashamed of myself now, with thoughts of the times I had preached to Kunle and even invited him to church on Sunday nights.

'Good news brother, guess who I met today! Rotimi Wellington, now Rotex Wells. The motherfucker is a big guy now. He owns a restaurant in the city and lives on Staten Island. You remember Rotex, the short dude who was always getting into fights and brawls with everyone.'

'Yeah, Rotex. I remember him. He was the one who poured hot water on a senior student and ran away from the hostel.'

I scratched my beard and pushed the beer bottle under a stool.

'That is the devil. I am in a team that will provide security for an event he is having before the opening of his restaurant. I had a chat with him privately and he asked to see us when I told him about you. I think he is gonna help you, dude.'

That was how Rotex Wells came into my life. I met with him and he offered me a job. He also helped work out my papers. I was to be his assistant and help supervise some of his staff. He liked the fact that I had banking experience which will be put to use. I moved into a nice apartment paid for by Rotex in the Southeast of Brooklyn, close to his home. I shared a two-bed flat with another member of staff and life seemed to be getting better. My work permit came in but I was told by my flatmate that it was fixed, as I could only use it to work for my new boss.

'For now, who cares? Just give me a job and forget stories man', I told my new flatmate, Mickey.

Laraba, who was in Nigeria, was not happy about the new job. She said something was not right when I called her weeks later.

'S.J, I can feel it. Something is not right about this guy. I wish I could lay my hands on it.'

'Be happy for me Labalaba. I am now living not existing. I have left that hellhole without hope. I am using my head now.'

I could not tell her what Mickey said about my fixed work permit. Neither could I tell her what Rotex said in my last discussion with him. His words echoed in my head again.

'Sanjay, you have to wake up in this country. Use your brain man. You are still tied to a woman at home. Do you know if another man is ...?'

'Not my woman, Rotex. She is an angel. You need to meet her.' I quickly cut in.

'Angels are in heaven man. I can work out some nice babes here for you. I am talking about some nice rich ass. All you need to do is show them you have divorced your wife, and then tie the knot here man. That's how I climbed up. I got my papers and became wise. We went our separate ways but I got out rich, man. I stash up money for five years as I was digging the old maid. She likes them black and strong, that thing between your legs. You can bet my man and I gave it to her every goddamn day.'

'I am okay for now, Rotex. I thank you for your help.'

'S.J, are you there?' I was jolted back to my phone call with Laraba.

'I am here dear. I am yours all the way. How are you coping without my arms around you on cold days?'

'You know I am okay. It is you that I am worried about. How are you coping S.J?'

'I am coping and holding on for you baby. Can you come over soon? It is almost a year now' I said in a low and unsure tone.

'I will work it out soon'. She then burst into tears.

She could not come for another year. Her visa application was rejected based on having no family ties to bring her back to Nigeria. It was apparent they knew I had gone to the U.S. and had not returned. She was emotionally down because she only wanted to see me and have no desire to remain in the States. She tried stopping me from going to the U.S. but I refused. I cried for two days behind closed doors and Rotex was sympathetic for once. He gave me a few days off and a loan to buy a used Toyota Highlander 2014 for her.

'Send it to her through my shipping agency. She will forget you when she gets this. Women love gifts.' He teased to cheer me up.

The car cheered her up but not for long. Appeals were made for the visa refusal and all of a sudden, she called; it had been granted! She was ecstatic and was in New York two weeks later. It was like we had never made love before. We were in each other's arms for days. Rotex gave me a two-week break and a free flight ticket to Mexico for an all-expense paid trip. I thought this would change Laraba's feelings about him but she was always cautious around him. She told me in private that she was suspicious of him. She kept asking if we were involved in some form of crime. I dismissed her claims and told her our businesses were legitimate.

Her four-week stay rekindled my spiritual life. I got closer to the church I had been attending and started discipleship classes. The assistant pastor and his wife visited us and I promised to enrol as a worker in the church. When the time came for her to go back home, I begged her to stay but she refused.

'S.J, we must prove them wrong. I am going back home. You know I will give up everything in the world to be with you, but I must go back. I will not overstay.'

'So, I am a sinner abi?'

'Not that S.J, but come back home. You have made some money. Come back home and start a business. You could even start a microfinance bank.'

'Sounds good, but what about government policies that are never stable, bad roads, insecurity, and poor power supply?'

'S.J, you have lived with that all your life and succeeded. The lay-off at the bank was just a temporary setback. If you had waited, I am sure something could have come up for you. You are not a pushover. With God on our side, we could have worked out something. Some of the people who left the job with you are picking up and moving on with life.'

'I was going crazy babe; I could have committed suicide. I was badly hit because I put all I had into that job. More so, I had no investment anywhere. The agribusiness with Kola and Ahmadu had gone bad. All my savings went into helping friends. Were they sincerely wrong? Was I swindled by my friends? Only God knows. I needed to get away from all that.' I stopped to breathe.

'And away from me too?' She said as she glowed under the moonlight on the balcony of my flat. The two-bedroom flat was all mine as Mickey, my flatmate, had moved to Chicago. We were above the street's lights. The moon was smiling at two lovers in the middle of soul searching. No birds sang here, the movement of cars on the streets below were the only sounds at that time of the day. A few crazy blaring horns could not distract us. She looked younger and slimmer.

'I am never far from you, my love. Every day I stayed away from you, I died and woke up. I never knew I would be faithful to you for two years.'

'Were you?'

'What? Did you just ask that? Tell me it was a slip of the tongue.' I tickled her and she stood up and ran into the sitting area. I ran after her and we ended up in each other's arms.

We cried and cuddled as I knew nothing will stop this woman with a heart of gold to stay. She was going back to prove the white men wrong, that not all blacks were criminals, frauds and unreliable.

I knew her music ministry was already blooming. She had immersed herself in music while I was away. She had enough time after work hours to put together a band and they have an album. The band was waiting for her return to start promoting the album. Two singles earlier released were making waves and climbing up the Christian music charts. The album was good and was a dream come through. She took some video shots in New York to add to her music video clip. She was also doing well at the ICT company she worked for. She was the assistant HR manager and was hoping to get promoted someday.

So, she went back home. I stayed at a restaurant close to the airport as I watched her plane take off two hours later and remembered one of my dad's favourite songs by John Denver; '*Leaving on a Jet Plane*' with a remix by Kris Okotie in the 80s. I searched for the track on YouTube and listened to it repeatedly. My pager buzzed and Rotex's voice boomed;

'Sorry lover boy, come back to work. We gotta make money.'

I drown my drink, paid the check and hit the road.

Two months later, Laraba sent me a text; "I am pregnant." I went berserk as if I was going mad. I remembered how I stuck to Laraba after NYSC. I was posted to a government agency that supervised construction works and this allowed me to meet with different people in Ibadan. I got information that a bank was recruiting and I applied. I went through different stages of tests and interviews at their assessment centres and came out as one of the best candidates. Two hundred people were employed out of thousands that applied.

Laraba was pressured to redeploy but she did not. Being the only girl in a family of four boys, she was her father's pet and he was very ill. I went to Jos twice with her to see her ailing father who had a good sense of humour. He was a devoted Christian and a deacon in his church. He asked if I was born again and if he could entrust his daughter to me. Deacon Bulus Ansa was a warrior who held on to Christ till his last breath. He passed away four months before our wedding. He insisted that in the event of his death, our wedding should not be cancelled. And so, we had the wedding. Laraba's oldest brother gave her away. It was a lowkey event because of the recent loss in the Ansa family.

Laraba was retained by the ICT firm she worked for during the service year. She was part of a team that developed software for a big client. This won bigger contracts for the firm and broke them into the industry's mainstream. We were both happy and upwardly mobile. We moved into our own home, a four-bedroom bungalow, about six years after we started working. Everything was going on well until the job loss.

Now, it seemed God has remembered us again. I was confused. I had waited for this all along and begged Laraba to come over. She only agreed to come for the delivery. This was because her band and ministry were doing very well and had won many awards. She had many singing engagements, interviews and television sessions for her album promotion. The music video was also a hit. I told her to slow things down now that she was pregnant and she assured me that she would be fine. I begged her mum to stay with her and she relocated to Ibadan that same week. This was a relief.

About this time, I noticed a lot of changes in Rotex. Funds were being transferred from the company's accounts to offshore accounts. He explained that he wanted to buy a big hotel abroad with some other investors and that the company was expanding. He also got into trouble with one of his girls who wanted either marriage or settlement. It was more of blackmail as she had many business documents stolen from him, including nude pictures of them together. I was livid and wondered how Rotex could be silly enough to allow her to get hold of our business transactions. Rotex was calm about the situation and said she was nothing to be bothered about.

True to his words, Sharon; for that was her name, disappeared into thin air. I asked what happened to her and he told me to ask the FBI. He hired a private security company for himself and started starving the business of funds. Some documents went only to him and when I asked for them, he told me not to bother.

This went on for months. Although salaries were paid promptly, I knew it was Laraba's fears about Rotex that were gradually coming to pass. I sensed trouble immediately. Where would I go? How could I move away from my benefactor? I wondered. I began sending more money to Laraba and I put more money in my domiciliary account in Nigeria, in case anything goes wrong. I was also sending cars and medical equipment to my younger brother in Nigeria who would sell them and move the proceeds into my account.

One night, I got a strange call from Laraba's mother;

'She is bleeding and it is heavy Sanjay', she said in a deep fearful voice. 'She did not want me to tell you but you need to know my son'.

Laraba had come back tired from one of her singing engagements and after a cold shower, she went to bed. She woke up to find her nightgown soaked in blood. She was taken to the hospital and was placed on bed rest but her blood pressure was not stable and no medication worked. When I spoke to the doctor, he said she had eclampsia and the high blood pressure was not responding to treatment. She had occasional seizures which scared me badly. I could not sleep. I had my brother's wife move in to assist her mother. I wish I was around to support and be with her.

It got to a point; I could not speak to her again because she was in a coma. I asked that she should be moved to a better and more expensive hospital because I felt she was not getting enough attention. I was no longer myself. I was going crazy, shouting at everything and everyone. I looked terrible with my unshaven beard. I couldn't take it any longer, so I told Rotex I was going home to my wife.

'Guy, you can go but remember that you have history here man. You will not find it easy to return with this new republican government coming into office'. He said distantly.

'Republicans are bad with immigration. You better stay man, she is gonna be okay.' After some time, he offered to help.

'We can hire an ambulance to bring her in. It's going to cost a fortune but I can work that out for you man', he said, with a lot of seriousness and concern. I scratched my overgrown beard and thanked him for his help. I would rather go. I didn't care about anything but Laraba.

He was not himself; I knew something was wrong and he was not willing to talk about it but at that time, I no longer cared. I booked my flight, handed my flat papers to Kunle and gave instructions in case I could not come back. I sold my car, emptied the account and sent part of the money to my brother while the rest was cleverly layered in my hand luggage.

Rotex had taught me a trick he often uses to move cash out of the country. I hoped it would work for me as well since no camera at the airport had ever caught him. It seemed my flight took forever and I wished I could fly in the wind to get to my love. I felt my presence would change everything and I looked forward to being present during delivery. The coma was just what bothered me. It was strange but I was hopeful that she would come out of it.

The taxi that took me from Lagos to Ibadan moved slowly and the driver was a chatterbox. I was forced to tell him to cut the talk and hit the pedals. Ibadan was changing, new structures were coming up and the city was getting neater. The road to Challenge, a popular area when coming in from Lagos was now a dual carriageway but the trading along the road was ubiquitous. Big billboards were everywhere.

The ride to the hospital was long and I got impatient as we crawled along. My WhatsApp call to Dehinde, my brother and his wife was not returned. I borrowed the driver's phone to call Mama, but her line was switched off. I headed straight to the hospital and did not care about my appearance after over eleven hours on air and two hours on the road. The taxi would wait for Dehinde to pick up my bags but I kept my hand luggage by my side always. I had escaped the airport security system with cash of twenty-five thousand dollars in my luggage. The Nigeria immigration officers at the airport gave no trouble as a hundred-dollar bill did the magic. I walked out of the airport with VIP treatment.

At the hospital, the receptionist refused to take me to Laraba.

'Has she been discharged?' I asked.

'Please wait to see the doctor. She will be here soon.'

'I will like the "soon" to be now, please. I need to see my wife.' I said as I banged on the table.

'Can we go to my office, Mr Ajayi?' A female voice asked me from behind.

I noticed that two members of staff followed us not too closely and stayed outside as we entered the doctor's office. It took her a few seconds to explain Laraba's ordeal.

'I will like to see her doctor. We can talk about all these later please?'

'I am sorry Mr Ajayi, we lost her and the baby.'

My world stood still at those words; the hours that followed were hell. I cried, screamed and even bite one of the attendants. I was wrestled to the floor by four men before I was given sedatives and placed in a ward for two days on intravenous fluid.

My whole life crashed. I hated everyone in the hospital and looked at them with disdain. They all seemed useless to me if they could not save a pregnant woman. What were they paid for? I kept asking no one in particular.

'Get me out of this death house before I strangle somebody.' My voice was murderous as I asked my brother to get me discharged from the clinic where Laraba had died.

I wish she had listened when I asked her to stay back in New York, where there was respect and value for life. I was also sorry for the millions of Nigerians trapped in a forsaken country where nothing has never nor will ever work. I checked into a hotel because I couldn't go home. Laraba would be everywhere in the house; her laughter, smell and orderliness would just stare me in the face at every corner.

Dehinde stayed with me at the hotel. I barely spoke and at some point, I felt sorry for him. He had become my emotional punching bag. He was very liberal about religion and God. I saw him sober, and reflective. And at times, he would be on the Bible App on his phone.

'You will be okay brother, yes you will be. Please stay strong.' He encouraged, looking at my heavily bearded face. Grey hair had sprouted from nowhere. Then I remembered Laraba's mother. The poor woman has had so much grief in such a short time; her husband and now, her only daughter.

'What of Mama Jos?', that was what we all call her.

'She is fine, I guess. She is with Edward', my brother replied.

I called her that afternoon.

'How are you, Sanjay? '

'I am not fine Mama. You know life is not worth it without Laraba.'

We remain silent as the clock ticked on at both ends. I knew she was trying to fight the tears. I ended the line and began to sob again. Dehinde could not hold back his tears too. As I ran, Dehinde ran after me and pulled me away from the door leading to the balcony, overlooking the car park that was five stories below.

After a week in the hotel, I moved in with Dehinde and his family. His children were my succour, especially his caring 4-year-old daughter who would sing for me till I slept. Nights were no longer peaceful as I stayed awake staring into space and listening to music without paying attention. I ate more and started gaining weight. I had not been to the gym in four weeks and had lost my well-toned muscles. I seldom went out until I was forced to get home supplies from the supermarket by my brother twice a month.

I refused to see the pastors brought to counsel me by Dehinde's wife. After the third attempt, I warned her sternly never to invite any prayer contractor to visit me again.

'I am just trying to help, Uncle. You need to get your life back. Life must go on sir'. She said with much concern.

I hissed and left for my room while banging the door after me. Later that day, I asked Dehinde to get me an apartment. I said I was doing okay and would not want to be a bother to him and his family forever.

'You do not want to go back to the states?' He asked.

'I am home for good', I answered.

The news of Rotex's disappearance after moving to Mexico came in from Kunle. Mexico was a crazy place. He must have secured a new passport with a different name.

'What about biometrics?' I asked Kunle.

'Biometrics doesn't work in the underground man. The IRS is after him and you are lucky to be out of the country too. I hope the Interpol will not come after you', he said.

There was nothing more to live for. Laraba was gone, Rotex had become non-existent and Interpol may be after me. What was the essence of all I had lived for? Life was not worth it. All the money in the bank was useless. Laraba's fame spread like wildfire after her death. She won a posthumous award as the gospel artist of the year. I accepted the award on her behalf and clutched it to my chest as if I was holding her again.

The days after these were horrifying. I did not want to speak to anyone. I stayed in my room with all the curtains down. Sunlight had become an intruder to the solitude I enjoyed thinking and speaking to Laraba. I kept the intruder away with the curtains down all day. Solape, Dehinde's wife brought food in and replaced it even when I don't touch it. Dehinde was going to Abuja for a conference and a mandatory improvement course. He asked me to come along for a change of environment but I declined. Three days after he had gone to Abuja, my plan was set.

The light flicker of the sun burned my iris. I tried lifting my hands to protect my eyes and adjust to the sunlight, but I could not. After about ten minutes, I adjusted to the light and saw myself in the hospital Laraba had died. The logo of the hospital was conspicuously embossed on the bed frames, bed sheets, television and everywhere. Will I ever escape from the horror of this place, from a world too cruel and filled with unending grief? My stomach churned. I turned to the other side, pulling the line from the intravenous fluid feeding my system. I tried to check which day it was. I must have been here for a week. How did they find me and why this hell of a place? I growled and groaned. Just then, the door opened and a nurse came in.

'Welcome back to life', she said.

I thought it was Laraba. They had the same voice but hers was not as high-pitched and soothing as Laraba's. I was tempted to call her by Laraba's pet name but stopped. Then she turned. She was petite, light-skinned and has a glow in her eyes. There was a strange calming aura around her.

'Back to hell', I muttered.

'Welcome back to a second chance.' She was now checking my pulse, eyes and blood pressure.

'Can you get me off this nonsense?' I said as I waved at the line.

'Not my call. The doctors will decide on that when they see you. Stay calm and be law-abiding.'

She had a down-to-earth and daring personality. Then I saw her name, Tito Alade, clearly written on the pin attached to her dress.

'I want to go home.'

'The doctors will decide that too.' With that, she moved out of the room.

My brother and the other family members visited later that evening after the doctors had allowed the intravenous lines to be removed. I was placed on fluids for the time being. They all had enquiring looks on their faces but nobody asked any questions.

The following day, a pastor visited me from Solape's church. She excused herself knowing fully well that I would be angry with her. The pastor sat awkwardly for some minutes before he started talking about God's love and why it was wrong for anyone to commit suicide.

I coughed in the middle of his sermon and switched to rancorous laughter.

'Love? Love! Where was that love, that God's love when Laraba, who kept herself until marriage, stayed faithful serving this God, was all over the place for God but could not bear a child? And when the child was to come, she lost her life and the baby. Love? Is that what you call love?' I sat up, confronting and shouting at the man of God.

'His ways are unsearchable. Job said in Chapter 23 verse 10 of the scriptures; "But He knows the way that I take; When He has tested me, I shall come forth as gold". You are meant to come out as gold. Wait on Him dear brother', the pastor counselled.

'If I am to come out as gold, what about Laraba?'

'She is in a better place. We knew her and we have been comforted that she is at the bosom of the Saviour. Why should you lose seeing and being united with her again?'

We talked for an hour but I was not in agreement that God had done right in this matter. I wished to leave this world and find rest in another clime. The pastor had said I was blessed to be back. He finally left me with nurse Tito who had taken over the shift.

'Do you think you have the monopoly of grief?' She asked in her no-nonsense manner. 'No one has the monopoly of joy too. Life happens and we move on trusting God for the best.'

I was shocked at her verbal brutality. She seemed to be the only unsympathetic one like she almost did not care if I was dead or alive. At first, I thought it was a "nurse" thing to be apathetic.

'If you must know, as you walk out of this hospital, you are walking into the police station for questioning on attempted suicide. Is it worth it?'

I just stared at her.

'It's my life,' I shrugged.

'I hope you don't end up in jail for wanting to take your own life. I also hope you know that suicide is an offence against the state.'

'Who cares?'

'Mister, so many people care about you but you want to die. Yes, you lost a beloved one but that's not the end of the world. God is still good and on the throne.'

'Spare me, nurse, don't tell me you are one of the "holy holy" ones. I have been there and I have come out with nothing'. I was adamant. 'You don't know my grief.'

She went to the door and turned the latch, locking the door from within. She removed her wig and said;

'I know this is unprofessional but you need to know life is beyond you', she moved closer. I stared at her head; her scalp bore scars of second-degree burns. Then I noticed that one of her ears had been burnt along with the scalp. My mouth was opened.

'This happened on my wedding day while coming back from the reception. After waiting for seven years to be married to my heartthrob who was in the U.S., I was to join him in less than a year. On our way from the reception, we got held up in traffic and all of a sudden, a fuel truck on the other side lost control and fell, spilling its content. A fire kindled as the fuel flowed in our direction. It was a moment caught in time. Everyone scrambled for their life. I lost all my family members including my husband for five hours. My only brother survived but had to spend a year in the hospital. I also had multiple surgeries before I could be here today.' She said, placing the wig back.

I was still speechless.

'I am still here and God is still good. We may face tribulations but He has promised us that He has overcome and we will also overcome. No one has the monopoly of grief or monopoly of joy.' She opened the door and turned to look at me. Her look pierced my heart like a sword.

I wiped away a tear as I sat up. Laraba is back!

FREE INDEED

The day was winding down as usual on a Thursday afternoon. It was regarded as a half-day by most business entities. This is because of the weekly environmental sanitation order from the state government. All businesses were mandated to clean their surroundings and it was reluctantly becoming a norm. However, small business owners use this period to laze around and get extra hours of sleep.

A heavy downpour resulted in a disastrous flood a few years ago in the city of Ibadan. It took many lives and rendered many homeless. This infamous episode led to the weekly environmental sanitation. Women use this period to clean their homes, especially those in the formal sector. Most men use it as a time to rest while catching up on their favourite television programmes.

For Adigun Benson, it was like any other day of the week except for Fridays with lesser workloads, a prelude to a weekend filled with church activities. He sat behind his desk at the state-owned science secondary school at Bashorun. He shared the office with the second vice-principal. He was reviewing the lesson notes of class teachers assigned to him for the coming week.

Mr Ojotide was always careless with punctuation. He carefully corrected errors in the teacher's manual and made comments on adjustments to be made.

He shook his head while hissing and muttered,' I hope he will not learn the hard way', as he put the last lesson note away.

Reviewing Ojotide's lesson note always comes last as he would not want to spoil his mood before reviewing other teachers' lesson notes.

He glanced at the wall clock as the school timekeeper rang the bell, indicating the close of work. The thought of his daughter who recently gained admission into the premier university in town flashed through his mind. He offered a silent prayer of thanks for being able to pay all the fees and get the young lady settled in the university. He knew he was on a tight budget until the next salary is paid. His wife, Adufe, was very cooperative in ensuring that basic things were provided for her.

He packed his bag, locked the office and moved to his car. The second vice principal will still come back to the office. His car had just been cleaned by the security guard, Suraj. Tomorrow, Friday is the payday for the unsolicited gesture. Suraj took his bag from the student who carried it and deposited it with other files on the back seat. Suraj brought two freshly plucked pawpaw and placed them in the back of the car. Benson knew that his weekly allowance to Suraj must increase.

He appreciated the guard and promised to see him the next day. Benson drove out of the school through large crowds of students on their way home. Mrs Prosper, the French teacher and her son were at the gate, waiting for a lift. He slowed down to offer them a ride home.

'Thank you, sir.' She expressed her gratitude as she settled at the back with her son and warned the boy not to step on the pawpaw.

As they drove, all sorts of merchandise were lined along their route. Horns blared at the playful and careless students on the roadside. Benson was now at the Idi-ape intersection where there was a park of motorcycle riders.

He drove the car towards the other side. Because the traffic warden was absent, caution was thrown to the wind. Just then, a car from the other side of the road accelerated towards them, ignoring the fact that he was halfway into the road, though maintaining its lane. A motorcycle called 'Okada' swerved from the right side of the road to cross to the left side. The car that had just accelerated rammed into the motorcycle, pushing it towards Benson's car. At that instant, the rider was lifted off the bike by the collision force and landed on Benson's car with a loud thud. Benson pressed the brake almost immediately, and the rider rolled down to the road, landing on his back with another impact to his head.

In an instant, Benson rushed out of the car to see the extent of the impact. A gash of torn flesh at the back of the head and another open flesh around the arms oozed out blood, the cream cotton shirt he wore showed the blood gushing out without restraint. Shouts and screams rented the air in a few seconds.

A retinue of motorcycle riders converged quickly, and a court of diverse opinions on who was guilty was immediately constituted. No doubt the riders' assembly would pitch their tent with their peer. As Benson looked down at the injured man, traffic was already brewing. Mrs Prosper shouted in disagreement, pointing to the other car that had not stopped, as the legion of riders tugged at the injured man. A passer-by pulled out his cell phone to take pictures, and he was joined by a few others.

At this time, Benson had squatted beside the rider and was trying to hold him down to a comfortable position. There were cuts all over the back of his head and he was bleeding from a deep gash on his arm. There was a cacophony of voices all around, accusing and exonerating at the same time.

'We need to get him to the hospital immediately', he said, rising to his feet. The man was now calm but groaning from the pain in his back.

Four men pulled the man up and took him to the back seat of Benson's car. A rider shouted that one of them should ride in the car so that Benson would not run away and that some other riders should accompany them to the hospital.

'Abeg make somebody go to the police station before these people will start speaking big English', a voice from the crowd advised.

'What about the man who hit the motorcyclist and ran away?' Mrs Prosper asked no one in particular as she held on firmly to her child.

By the time they got to the hospital, the man had stopped groaning and everyone was scared for his life. The nurses at the hospital carried him in while the riders held on to Mr Benson, accusing him of murder. Twenty minutes later, a policeman was brought in from Iwo Road and Benson was invited to the police station to make a statement about the event. Benson at this point was in a daze. He drove the police and two other riders to the police station.

Mrs Prosper went to get help for her vice principal. Benson started praying under his breath as he was a lone voice in the midst of accusing fingers. He was stripped of all valuables after giving his statement at the station and put behind the officer's counter.

'But officer, the hit-and-run driver is the offender. He hit the man and pushed him to my car. I should not pay for being a sincere and caring Nigerian', Benson said to the officer who was busy logging in the incident in the crime register.

He simply looked at him, shook his head and continued writing in the register.

'The other car hit the man and pushed him to my car. He ran away. I stayed because I value life. I did not hit him, officer. These people were not at the scene', he repeated.

'No problem, Mr Benson. You will stay here until the man comes around to declare your innocence, that is if he is not dead', the police officer replied finally.

Benson shivered at the thought of the man never coming back to life.

The events thereafter were unimaginable for Adigun Benson. The divisional police officer was a surly and obnoxious fellow. He was angry at everyone and everything. He ordered that Benson be locked up in the local cell at the station. The school principal, who had come with Benson's wife and his younger brother the following day, asked for bail but was denied because it was a weekend. Bails could not be processed until the next working day, which was Monday.

Benson was in for long, sad and gruelling days in the cell. The cell was 14 by 12 feet, meant to hold a maximum of four men awaiting trial. At the moment, it was holding ten men. The smell of sweat and urine welcomed Benson. As he tried to adjust his sight to the dimly lit room while trying to avoid stepping on men on the floor, something hit him on the head. It was a blow and then another landed on him. He covered his face quickly to protect his eyes and went down to the floor. He remembered his training on how to protect vital organs at the boy's scout in the event of an assault.

'Stop! You want to kill him?' a shout came from a corner.

The beating stopped as if it was controlled by a remote. He could taste blood in his mouth. One of the blows had hit him on the jaw and shifted his teeth to bite a lip. He sucked his lip.

'Welcome to the kingdom of Okuri inside Idi-Ape police station. I am Kingsley Dino, the unofficial landlord of this territory'. The booming voice declared.

'Respect' chorused the nine other voices.

The other nine men introduced themselves and their unofficial positions in the kingdom. Benson was asked to introduce himself and he did.

'That was a welcome party into the kingdom. Our tradition is that any new citizen of our kingdom throws us a party. So, it is your turn to feed this kingdom. If you are unable to feed us, you will become the servant of all.' Kingsley, who spoke fluently, explained to Benson.

'How do I get the money to feed everyone? All my belongings have been taken,' Benson explained.

'You no get family? Will they not visit you? Nonsense! If you do not feed us, there will be a problem.' One of the inmates replied with a gruff.

'Read the rules', Kingsley growled.

'Rule number one; No sodomy in this kingdom except by permission. Ashawo can be organised if you pay the bills. Rule number two; You can only defecate once a day between five and six in the morning and urinate twice a day. Rule number three; For every income, you pay a tax of ten percent to the landlord, ten percent to DPO, ten percent to station officers and thirty percent to the house.'

The two days Benson spent in the cell were horrific. He questioned God and lamented on what he could have done wrong to deserve such treatment. He reminded God of how faithful he had been with paying his tithe and all the good works he had done in God's house. He prayed mostly for release and kept to himself while abiding by the rules of the cell. He was released on Monday evening. While waiting for his release to be processed, he learnt that the bike rider had regained consciousness and had given a statement that Benson was not the one that hit him.

The police delayed his release as five young men from a bank were brought in for fraud. He recognised three out of the five men. They were staff of the bank that operates the school's account. One of the young men was Sayo George, whom he had grown to love and admire for his humble and Christian disposition.

Sayo appeared calm, but he had a streak of worry in his eyes as they sat close to Benson.

'What happened sir?' He asked.

Benson explained the situation to Sayo who seemed less worried than the other colleagues.

'All things work together for those who love God and are the called according to His purpose', Sayo said.

'I know the Lord is with me and will keep me even when I walk through the valley of the shadow of death. Pray for me as you go home, sir.' Sayo continued as he was taken away with the other men.

Sayo and the other staff were taken to the cell and they went through the welcome party as Benson did. It was a bitter experience for the bank staff as they were not familiar with the rough life of those criminals. Sayo came out with a sprain on his arm. He was taken to the hospital the next day after the DPO inquired about the reception party and how it got out of hand. Kingsley, the leader in the cell, was punished and some inmates were relocated to smaller cells to reduce the tension in the large cell. The bank staff received beatings because the inmates felt they had money and should be able to bribe their way out.

Kingsley Dino, Sayo with two other cell mates ended up in the same cell. The four were quiet at the initial stage. Kingsley, also called 'Okuri', was the first to speak.

'What happened in the republic is just natural. Don't hold it against anyone.'

He spoke fluently unlike his usual pidgin.

'It was a welcome party that went too far. The DPO and the officers all know that we usually have the party for fun and to raise money.'

He explained to Sayo as Smallie, one of the other inmates stood behind Kingsley, fanning him using his shirt.

'Tell me about yourself and what brought you here. Remember, no lies. Make you talk better o.' He switched to pidgin.

'I am the last child in my family but lost my father in my first year in secondary school. It was not easy for my mother to raise four children by herself as a primary school teacher. It was tough and being a religious woman, she took me to church all the time. It was rough for my older siblings than I. They had to sell petty things on the streets for our mother to get additional income for the family. By the time I almost finished secondary school, I had become a church boy in a Pentecostal church. I became a part of the church campus fellowship when I gained admission into the university. The campus provided financial support for its students. I was a beneficiary and this eased my stay in the university.'

He paused for breath, then continued:

'NYSC was a wild time, I lost control and got into some bad companies but my Christian upbringing never left. I tried to come back to God whenever I veered off. I got involved with some boys who were into pretty bad things; partying, girls, booze, drugs and internet scams. After the service year, I went home to the church and my heritage. Through one of the elders in the church, who was a banker, I was able to get a job as a contract staff.'

'Life changed as I got the job after youth service. Though the job was exhausting, it was financially rewarding for a fresh graduate like me. I got back to church and was serving as much as my job could allow. Then one day, a guy I had known from NYSC came into town, looked for me, and offered me a deal to defraud one of the bank's dormant accounts. After so much pressure from the guy and his syndicate, I gave in and here we are. We were caught.'

'How much was involved?'

'Twenty million naira', Sayo replied.

The other three men whistled in unison.

'How many of you were involved?' 'Four'

'But I thought you said you went back to church and was serving God?' Kingsley asked.

'Yes, things are not as they seem. Tell me about yourself too. You speak good English. Are you educated?' Sayo asked, diverting the attention from himself.

'I have been here for two years and will be going to court for a murder or manslaughter case, whichever you prefer. I was in my final year at the Polytechnic when it happened. My older sister was engaged to a guy. He was a smooth talker and a good spender. I guess she was in love and did not see him for who he was; a player. He proposed marriage and she accepted. She was the first child but our younger sister was married. She had a fairly good job in a manufacturing company. I have another younger sister. Our parents are working middle-class citizens.' Kingsley explained.

'The wedding date was fixed and it was to be a small affair. On that day, this bastard failed to appear at the registry. The whole family was thrown into disarray. My sister ended up in the hospital and had to be heavily sedated. I was angry with him because he had ridiculed the whole family and sent my sister into depression. I am an only son with three sisters and felt obliged to defend and fight for my sister.'

He continued; 'After she came back from the hospital, she tried committing suicide. I was fuming and wished I could lay my hands on the swindler who had messed her up. I was known as a quiet boy at home but in school, I got mixed up with some guys in a group. You may call it a cult; our main focus was to protect our members from other rival groups and guard our territory. My association with the group had made me tough and I was capable of anything.

The authorities of the school worked underground with us but would deny our existence. Some lecturers and senior staff members are our patrons and we do their bidding when needed. You can guess they watch our backs too.' He stopped for a breath.

'I felt like calling the group in to deal with this guy but I wanted to handle it alone. Also, it was not in the school territory.'

He continued, 'I remembered the guy once took me to a club with his friends at Bodija. I went there to confront him about what he had done. When I got there, he was with his friends and one over-bleached and over-made-up harlot by his side. I waited at another table in the dark for him to exit the club so I could face him alone. After a few drinks, I got crazy, went to his table and shouted at him, and a fight ensued. I broke a bottle over his head and he tried to fight back. In the scuffle, his head hit the edge of a table and that was it. He ended up in the hospital and never recovered. He passed on and I now have a death on my hands.'

'Sad, very sad' Sayo said, leaning on the wall.

'I have been in and out of court for two years now and no concrete judgement has been passed. I have not been transferred to a prison with the help of my uncle and I have become the landlord here. This place has made another man out of me. You need to be tough to survive here. It is clear where I am going; it is either a life-or-death sentence.'

There was silence between them.

'We all make mistakes. We want a better deal in life but clearly, we can't save ourselves. There is a saviour whom God has sent to heal our soul and deliver us from ourselves.'

Sayo used the opportunity to talk about forgiveness and mercy that comes from belief in Jesus. The three men listened attentively to the young man because his words had power. They did not know why, but they listened.

A new movement started in that cell. The four men sang and prayed every morning. The DPO noticed the peace in the cell and refused to move Kingsley back to the larger cell. Kingsley received sad and shocking news a few days later; his mother had passed away. He was in deep shock and his tears were uncontrollable.

Sayo stayed close and spoke comforting words to him. It was during this period he told Kingsley if he wanted to see his mother again, he should give his life to Christ.

Kingsley had been telling everyone that his mother was a very good Christian and that his prison ordeal was a shame and a blow to her faith. Sayo and the three men prayed together after Kingsley accepted to follow the Saviour.

Two days later, the five-bank staff were handed over to an anti-fraud investigating unit of the police force. Kingsley and Sayo lost contact briefly but Kingsley had a visitor from Sayo's church. He introduced himself as Elder Bosun and was the head of the church ministry to prison inmates. A bible and some Christian materials were given to him. All enquiries about Sayo from Kingsley were unanswered. The church team was consistent in visiting and when a life sentence was passed on Kingsley, he was transferred to the Federal Correctional Facility at Agodi. The church team was very supportive, but Sayo was nowhere to be found.

One year later, Kingsley was in high spirits as it was a visiting day and he was sure that his family would come as well as somebody from Sayo's church. He was neatly dressed and walked towards the visitor's waiting area after he had been called to receive his visitors. One of the inmates hailed him as a pastor, that was what he was called now. He had been transformed into a gentle, easy-going person and was now one of the leading figures in the prison Christian fellowship meetings.

As he approached the visiting area, he sighted his father and younger sister, with Elder Bosun and another male figure with a familiar build. He was dressed in a light blue shirt over a pair of black denim trousers. His beard hid the lower part of his face. But as he moved closer; the face became more like Sayo's. He had gained some weight and looked lighter in complexion. Kingsley stood with his mouth opened and let out a muffled scream as he ran into the arms of his friend. They embraced for about twenty seconds, looked at each other and embraced again.

'Where have you been my friend?' Kingsley asked.

'It's a long story', he said as they sat down.

'I am sure you have met my father and sister. They have been here with Elder many times. He must have introduced them.' He said holding his father and patting the sister by the shoulder. 'Papa, this is the man who spent a few days with me and changed the course of my life. He started it and handed me over to Elder who came in to ground me in faith. He has been the one who followed up and kept nurturing me.'

'All the glory to God' Elder said while Sayo beamed with a smile.

Kingsley looked transformed from the angry and distraught man Sayo met over a year ago. He now has a peace that was beyond understanding. He was neat, clean-shaven and fresh. His family and the church had provided much support for him and his positive attitude had endeared him to the wardens.

His involvement in the prison fellowship and skills acquisition centre had improved his relationship between the inmates and the authorities. He has a life sentence but appeals had been filed.

'So, tell me, where have you been?'

'I have been in Ghana this past year. Remember the fraud case? I was the whistle-blower. I could not bite the fingers that fed me. I reported the plot to my mentor, who asked me to play along as directed by the detectives. I was to go through the process so that all the members of the syndicate could be nabbed.

No money was lost as all the receiving accounts were frozen. The members of the gang were picked up and to remain unsuspected, I had to be arrested also and pushed around for a few days while every connection and godfather was arrested. As part of the police protection programme, I had to move out of the country. The bank gave me a permanent job in the office in Ghana. I am on a few days' vacations and thought it would be nice to see you.' Sayo explained as he paused for breath.

Kingsley listened intently and nodded as Sayo finished speaking.

'You have heard about the case, my friend. Whatever it is, I am not afraid of death. I have met the author of life. Though in chains, and behind bars, I have been set free. I am free indeed because the son of God has set me free.'

They huddled together and offered a prayer as the warden came to announce that visiting time was over.

Sayo went back to Ghana a few days later but kept in touch with Kingsley while the appeal was ongoing. He later got engaged to Kingsley's younger sister. The older sister who was jilted met a widower, a medical doctor living in Canada who had come home to find another wife. Within six months, they were married and three months later, she joined him in Canada. Kingsley continued to maintain a positive attitude regardless of whatever happened in court. He was sure of making heaven, having met the author of life.

BODIJA AVENUE

The Toyota corolla weaved out behind a compact Nissan Micra car used in the ancient city of Ibadan and many towns in the Southwest as taxis. It was touted as efficient in fuel conservation and thus became the choice for the taxi business.

The driver behind the wheels sighed deeply and restrained himself from making any comment or cursing as the taxi driver halted at the sight of a prospective passenger. It was before a UBA branch on Bodija main road, after Awolowo junction. As usual, the road was busy around GTBank as the traffic wardens; three in number were more interested in favours than controlling the traffic.

Duke, who was behind the wheels, was listening to the news update at 1 pm on Fresh FM radio station, owned by a musician and broadcaster. He was a fan of the station. By his assessment, the station has a balanced approach to news, information and entertainment. He drove past some eateries and noted that on his way back, he might have to pick up a lunch pack at Foodco supermarket.

He turned left to Bodija Avenue, previously known as Osuntokun. It was not a busy street at the moment but from experience, it is a beehive of activities at night, a haven for night crawlers and debauchery seekers. As he drove to his destination, he remembered the meeting with his editor the day before.

Demola Smith sat behind a large desk with his protruding pot belly, a sign of too much alcohol. He has two weaknesses; alcohol and women. He had stopped trying after three failed marriages and had resigned to enjoying any woman he fancied. He never admits to being a saint but also believed that no woman was an angel. His closeness with Duke developed out of respect for each other's brilliance and professional knack for excellence. Demola had won numerous awards as best editor of the year just as Duke had won laurels for reporting and investigative journalism.

'Have you noticed the rising cases of rape and juvenile defilement in the news? And abuse of young boys by older males?'

Demola asked as he tapped on his desk while eyeing the news flash on the muted television.

'Yes, I have.' Duke replied.

'There is a gay community in this city. I want you to dig up stories about them. It might shed more light on the rising cases of abuse of the male gender.'

'Why me, Edi?' Duke asked, using the name everyone called him as the editor.

'You applied to work in this goddamn publishing house, Duke! Wake up, man. The month will end soon and you will be checking your account for your salary. Work for the money you earn mister.' He teased back.

'Seriously, you know this is not my turf.'

'Make it your turf guy and spare me the bullshit. Money talks and bullshit work. Let's start chopping wood, my friend'.

Demola scribbled a number on a paper and pass it to him.

'That guy will drive you closer to the gist. I want to know what is behind this fad. I want the story on the front page of the weekend special on Saturday. Good luck pastor and God bless you.' He joked as he reached for his phone that had been ringing.

Duke left the office of his boss and editor. The walls have several awards belonging to the publishing house, Demola and other staff members. Demola had worked abroad for a while after schooling in the United States.

His first marriage was to an American lady whom he left for an African-American. He claimed she had a better physical build and could withstand his aggression. Demola ran back home after he was caught with another woman by the African-American lady, who pulled a gun on him.

He had not gone to the States ever since, although the lady had repented and was pregnant for him. She had the child and he is now a teenager. Demola has the picture of his son displayed like a badge on his desk. The boy was a split image of him. Demola was one of the founding editorial staff of the newspaper outfit; *DAILY TRUTH*. He grew to be the editor after seventeen years of meritorious service and loyalty to the management and board.

Duke stopped the car in front of a shop that sells items to the residents in the neighbourhood. The lady behind the counter was busy with some calculations on her record book. Duke parked in an open space near the shop. There was a group of students playing in the open space before heading home from school.

The girls sang;
Bodija ko di ja
Ija ya, dide dide.
Ise ya, dide dide.

Oja ya, dide dide.
Bodija ko di ja.

Duke watched as the girls sang and the boys simulated a fight to gain control of the land and hand it over to the girls. He watched keenly as the little ones reprised the essence of the genders in their quest for life and living. He smiled and got down from his car. He approached the shop and requested a cola drink. After he paid and took a sip, he engaged the woman in conversation.

'I am looking for a club around here.' Duke started.

'There are a lot around this street. Half of the houses have been turned into clubs. It is sad. When you come at night, you would not recognise this place,' she explained.

'Number X23 Bodija Avenue would be the address.' Duke noted further.

'Ah! That is it over there,' she pointed as she sighed and shook her head.

Duke finished his drink and tossed the bottle into the trash can. He moved towards the direction she had pointed to. The house looked like a residential building. The fence hid the expanse of land and trees planted in the compound. It was once owned by a wealthy cocoa exporter. He made his money by buying cocoa when the price was low and selling to the international market when the price was high.

Akande Onikoko was a known socialite who had three wives and many concubines. After his death, the family sold the house and shared the proceeds. The current owner was the fifth person to own the house. His children abroad leased it for ten years, hoping to get a better value for it in future.

Duke stood in front of the building which had become like other buildings in the neighbourhood. Parents with houses in the government reservation area were the elites who could afford overseas study for their children. Many of these children opt to remain abroad rather than come back to Nigeria. They find the country "unprogressive" and underdeveloped. Because of this, their parents' houses are being sold or leased for commercial purposes.

The building was a massive twelve-bedroom duplex with en suite toilets and bathrooms. There was a swimming pool on the right side of the house with a terrace overlooking it. The left side of the building had a three-bedroom guest chalet. The servant quarters were behind the building. One couldn't see much outside the compound aside from these structures. Duke walked away without attracting attention from the security guard who sat lazily at the entrance, punching a cheap mobile phone.

Later that night, at 8:00 pm, the street had been transformed into a beehive of activities by night crawlers. Spillover of cars from the compounds was on both sides of the road. It was evident that the street has few residential buildings. The buildings which were not used for commercial activities during the day had been turned into nightclubs, bars, betting centres and sports viewing centres.

Duke was dressed in a cream-coloured turtleneck sweater on a pair of brown trousers and a jean jacket, with a pair of dark glasses. He had a pen in his pocket and his car keys in his hand. Demola had linked him with someone who would get him into the club. The escort was paid heavily by the newspaper. Demola usually handles such things with funds from the public relations budget. He had been warned not to come with cameras, phones or any recording device, and that the club only accept cash.

He brought two devices that only secret service agents can detect on him. His escort had given him a description of where to meet and what he would be wearing. He saw him from a distance and moved towards him. His code name for the night was Sylvester.

'Sylvester?' His escort asked as he drew closer.

'Yeah, man.' He answered. The thought of his job as both exciting and dangerous flashed through his mind. However, he had a refuge in God and He had never failed him.

They shook hands in the agreed way and hugged, in case someone was watching. They held each other and moved towards the entrance. The entrance had two hefty men at the pedestrian gate. He had been told not to park inside the compound as it was easier to saunter out and drive off.

The escort had assured him that he would be in the background and will be available to rescue Duke in case of any emergencies. The bouncer checked the escort's membership pass and then whisked them in with a metal detector. He also patted their body for any prohibited devices.

As they moved into the compound, they were ushered into a gangway, paved in concrete and roofed in asbestos sheets. There were multicoloured lights scattered all around to give the compound the look of a discotheque. The lights make facial recognition difficult. Music was coming from different directions. Duke glanced towards the swimming pool and saw that there were groups of people around the pool as a large barbecue party was going on there.

'The bar and main section are where pick up is.' The escort said as they moved through the small crowd at the entrance.

Michael Jackson's *'Dirty Diana'* had just ended as another song, *'They don't care about us'* started to play. The track was generating energy in the hall. Two guys swirled to the beats as they moved into the dancing area and a small crowd cheered them on.

They moved to the end of the room away from the DJ and had a vantage point of the stage. On both sides of the stage were poles painted with rainbow colours.

Duke took a sip of the non-alcoholic wine he ordered. As the smell of cigarettes filled the air, he prayed for a quick escape from there. Job, his escort, told him to relax and get ready to be taken. He sauntered off, greeting friends and exchanging banters as he went.

Duke looked around and realised it was a gay club in the city of Ibadan. Music, dance, drinks and flirting filled the air. The tempo of the beat became slow as Michael Jackson's rock track; '*Give in to me*' filled the air. A lady and her partner started an erotic dance on the dance floor. Two dancers, a male and a female, appeared on stage scantily dressed. They moved towards each pole, holding and cuddling it while strip dancers moved to the base of the stage. Few people already brought out naira notes and were waving them in the air. It was obvious they want the dancers to strip after throwing notes at them. They could also have them for the night if they can afford it. Duke watched with amusement and remembered Sodom.

A man knocked on his table, bringing him back to the present. The man wore a pink shirt with yellow trousers and a multi-coloured scarf wrapped around his neck. On his wrist was a brown and black bracelet with red and yellow beads dangling on the end. He was a little plump and had the waist of a woman. His lips had a glossy coating.

'May I?' He asked, pointing to the chair.

'Please do.' Duke offered the seat as he stood in courtesy. He knew this guest was to be treated like a lady.

'You are new.' He said, calling for the waiter.

'Yes, and no. I come often when I am in town.' He lied, as the waiter took the order. 'Please add that to my bill', he instructed. The waiter nodded and moved away. Duke paid for the drink as they turn to each other after watching the stripers who were now half naked, with naira notes littering the entire stage.

'It is Wacko Jacko night. I adore him. He was not fit for this world. I think he was much better out of it but he left us relics of his soul, a beautiful soul.' Duke's guest said as he took a sip from his glass of beer.

'You have not told me your name. I am Sylvester.' Duke said.

'Kris Madu.' He said, spelling the Kris to clarify it was not "Chris". 'Are you free or single?', he asked further, leaning forward to show the unbuttoned part of his chest.

'My friends call me Sly for short.'

Kris Madu was talkative and the beer was fuel for more talk. He asked if Duke wanted a pick for the night and was willing to pay. Duke agreed that he was up for it. Kris took him to the garden to discuss. This was where the first stage of romance started for couples. Men were making out with men and women were intimate too, they were not bothered about who was close by. Everyone was in his or her world. Kris fitted well into Duke's plan because of his talkativeness.

Kris asked Duke if he was open or in the closet. Duke said he was in the closet as he was married with two kids.

'How long will that be? Live your life man and enjoy your walk. If you are gay, you are gay. You can never live well in both worlds.' He said with pride. He went on to talk about how he became gay without Duke asking. Duke was glad he had a good subject.

Kris Madu grew up in Jos with his parents. His father was a low-ranking officer who was dismissed from the army. He ended up as a security guard and spend all his income on alcohol and gambling. His father had six children and was drunk each night. His mother was his punching bag and after the battery, he would beg to sleep with her. He does this loudly and all the children were the audience of the ignominy. Kris grew up wanting to leave home. He was always in and out of school, being sent home for lack of books or delayed payment of fees.

A neighbour asked his parents to allow Kris to become his assistant after school hours. The man sells plumbing materials and promised to send Kris to school. His parents agreed and he began living with Okechukwu, who was called Okey by everyone.

After his secondary school education, Okey told his parents of his intention to take Kris to Ibadan, where he had secured better business prospects. The riots in Jos and the fire outbreak at the Terminus main market, which left many traders with huge losses caused the relocation. Kris's parents agreed to the proposal. At Ibadan, Okey had to stay with a friend who was into the sales of electrical materials. They shared a room and Kris had to sleep on a mat. He served the two businessmen. Linus was a pornography addict and he initiated Okey. It became their past time at the close of work each day. Linus also smoked cigarettes, including weed. When he has money, he would bring in girls and lock Okey and Kris outside.

Okey had gone to Lagos on a Friday, to purchase new stocks and could not make it back that day. Kris was left with Linus who was disappointed by his date. He forced Kris to watch porn with him and thereafter, taught him how to give a blow job. This became a weekly affair and Okey was also pulled in by Linus. Kris became their slave both at work and in bed. This went on for many years until they each got married. They gave Kris the capital to set up a business. He kept the secrets of both men and was still at their service anytime they wanted to get away from their wives. Both men have become wealthy and Kris was also doing well.

However, Kris had been permanently damaged. He never had the desire for a woman but was at the beck and call of any man who would dominate and pay a fee for his services. Though he was a successful trader, he could never leave the life he had been sold into.

'The names I gave you are not their real names. But don't ask me for their names.'

'Are you saying this was not your choice?' Duke asked.

'I am who I have become', Kris said, using his left hand to brush his jerry curled hair which Duke just noticed.

'Tell me about yourself. I like hearing everyone's story.' Kris inquired.

Duke relayed one of the stories he had read somewhere as his story and this got Kris nodding. A couple walked towards them and Duke squinted as he looked closely. The gait of the slender male seemed familiar. Kris greeted the couple and hugged the slender one while the short sturdy guy slapped his bum. He pretended as if nothing happened. After the men had gone towards the pool; Kris told their story.

Kola Martins, the shorter man was about fifty years old. He was a banker who climbed the ladder of success fast, and many people claimed it was because he was bisexual. He was the personal assistant to an American executive director who was also bisexual. Kola was a sharp dresser when he was young. The American saw the raw ambition of Kola for success. He promised to help convert him to the banking sector if he would play his game. Kola agreed and became his bedmate. The American, Curtis, fulfilled his promise and Kola began climbing the corporate ladder. Kola got married but was living large with Curtis's image and money. He also began to sleep with Curtis's wife and daughter. After a dirty deal and lots of blackmail, Curtis sold his stake in the bank to Kola, who became the director while Curtis moved out of the country to save his family. Curtis committed suicide seven months later.

After years of scheming and more dirty deals, Kola became the managing director. But due to a lack of tact and a long line of enemies, he was pushed out of the bank but still, his stake in the bank remained intact. He returned to Ibadan where he was able to start a brokerage firm that dealt in financial services and shares brokerage.

Kola Martins built part of his business around Nigerians in the Diaspora. One of his clients was a male model, Leo, based in the United Arab Emirates. Kola fell not only for the young model's money but also for his body. Leo was well-travelled and had worked with some of the finest modelling agencies in the world. Kola used Leo's network to build his business. Leo started asking for more; a stake in the business and for Kola to be his manager. He also wants Kola to leave his family and move to UAE with him. Simply put, he wanted Kola to come out about his status. Many believe this would never happen as Kola was a rattlesnake. Behind the facade of a perfect successful pair, there was much pressure between them and Kris ended their sordid tale.

'Leo is in town for the Ibadan fashion week. He is one of the major promoters. You know his mother is from Ibadan and his father is from the Kogi state.

'Yeah, we got to move now', Duke stood up, paid the bill and left a tip for the waiter.

The ride to the hotel in the rented car was quiet. It was the hotel used by the gay community for short visits. It was known for privacy and efficiency in handling the police. Duke paid for the room in cash and requested that drinks be brought up. While Kris was in the bathroom, the drinks arrived and Duke paid for them.

He was tensed up at this point. He thought of what to do at this crossroads between professionalism and conviction. Should he just walk away? What he heard was enough for a good story but would he ever forget that he had an opportunity to reach out to a soul in need and he never did? He paced while Michael Bolton; '*How am I supposed to live without you*' track played softly in the background.

He removed his jean jacket and dropped it on the sofa. He almost reached for the drink but went for water instead. The DVD player played another track by the same singer. Kris came in, wrapped in the bathrobe of the hotel. He was naked underneath but for his boxers.

'Shower for you?' He asked as he sat at the edge of the bed.

'No,' Duke said as he sat on the chair, a little far from the bed.

Duke took a deep breath and said; 'Have you ever thought a change is possible?'

'Change? Change from what to what?' Kris asked.

'Listen to this', Duke opened Gideon's bible on the desk and read Romans 1:27; "Likewise also the men, leaving the natural use of the woman, burned in their lust for one another, men with men committing what is shameful, and receiving in themselves the penalty of their error which was due."

'From this Kris, there is a judgement awaiting this kind of life. God did not create you like this. Run away from the judgement that is coming.'

Hear again, '"He who overcomes shall inherit all things, and I will be his God and he shall be My son. But the cowardly, unbelieving, abominable, murderers, sexually immoral, sorcerers, idolaters, and all liars shall have their part in the lake which burns with fire and brimstone, which is the second death."

Kris sat on the bed staring at Duke. He gently placed the gel that was in his hand on the side locker.

'Jesus said in Revelation 3:20; Behold, I stand at the door and knock. If anyone hears My voice and opens the door, I will come into him and dine with him, and he with Me.' Duke stopped to draw in some breath.

There was an eerie silence. Their eyes locked as both men stare intently at each other.

'There is forgiveness with God through Jesus. He can deliver you from this life. Jesus can give you a new lease on life. He can give you a much more beautiful life.' Duke continued.

'Get out!' Kris simply said in a steel, cold voice.

Duke got up, picked up his jacket and walked out, closing the door gently behind him. He sighed as he took the elevator and got to the lobby. He felt a heavy load of guilt had just been lifted off his soul. After picking up his car from the club car park, he rode home on the deserted streets.

It was Eddy's call that woke him in the morning; 'Do you have another job elsewhere?' He shouted from the other end.

'Yes. Sleeping after a crazy night in hell' he teased back.

'Did you come across anyone named Leo Agbo, a model based abroad in your romp yesterday?' He asked, ignoring his wit.

'Yeah, what about him?'

'Dead, found stabbed in five places in his hotel room this morning. He is rumoured to be gay'. Eddy narrated without any emotion.

'I have some good stuff on him but I have to sleep now boss before I can give them to you', Duke said sleepily then thought to himself, 'Kola Martins was with Leo last night.' Big story!

'I want the stories on my desk by 3:00 pm. The editorial meeting is at five. Good luck Jonah.' Eddy blared back from the phone.

'How did you escape the U.S. immigration service?' Duke asked wryly.

'Ask your mum' and the line went dead.

LAZARUS

The crowd was fairly small today. They were usually under the trees around the house. Some would sit by the heap of clay under the fig and almond trees, while the trouble makers would prefer to be aloof, watching and armed with sticks under the olive trees. At the earlier times, the quiet crowd would enjoy time with Lazarus who would come sit with them and recount stories of how the Lord raised him after four days of being dead.

At other times, he would tell them stories about how Jesus preached and healed the sick. Then some, especially the younger ones, would ask questions. Because Lazarus had a deep soothing voice, he would sing for them and his friend, Josiah, would play the harp.

When some of the Lord's twelve were around, he would be in the background as they spoke to the people or prayed for their healing. Martha would then give bread and nuts to the young one. These had been going on daily for months after the Lord's death. The crowd had come to join the believers and were with the followers of the Lord. The chief priest heard this and sent a band of men to disperse them. They claimed Lazarus was never dead and was deceiving the people. He was just in a coma or had slept longer than Jonah, they said.

The crowds were few today as there were rumours of Lazarus getting arrested for forgery and for lying about his death. Some said the high priest will treat him the way the Master was treated. As the night drew near, the crowd started to disperse; the younger ones first, followed by the older ones.

Martha peeped through the small window to access the situation outside. She wrapped her scarf tightly around her head, sighed and moved into the inner part of the house. The cooking area had low embers of coal, giving a warm effect to the meal on the earthenware stove. She moved towards the stove and pulled back more dying embers.

As usual, Mary was with Lazarus, their brother. Both of them reminded her of their parents. People say Mary was the exact image of their mother; Eucharis. Her skin was smooth like hers with an almond-shaped face. Her soft voice was always disarming and begging. Only a few people could resist her pleading voice. Lazarus was tall like their father, Cyrus; with his large hands. Their mother said their father was responsible for the way Lazarus and Mary had turned out. He never scolded them for any wrong. Martha was the second child; Lazarus was older and Mary was younger than her.

As she got to them, the oil lamp cast its shadow on the wall. They looked up as she settled on a wooden stool beside them.

'The crowd is going home.' She said as she rested on the wall beside her.

'Oh, thanks be to Yahweh and His son. There will be no fights tonight.' Mary replied in appreciation.

'Any word yet from John?' Martha asked.

'Not yet, do not worry sister. All will be well. There is no harm.' He turned the last words into a song. Mary smiled and rose to waffle to the song.

'Stop Mary! You know the chief priest can do anything and the Roman leaders will look away. I do not want any harm to come to Lazarus.' She said with a voice laced with anguish.

Mary sat next to her, held her hands, and rubbed them against hers. Martha was like her mama; caring and strong as iron. She would never allow any evil to come near either of them. Like a mother hen, she was always looking out for them although Lazarus was the older one.

'Let me bring your food' Mary said as she stood. Martha, as was her custom, also stood and followed Mary. She knew Mary was trying to stop her from worrying about Lazarus's life-threatening. Lazarus hummed a song as the sisters brought the food. He placed three stools against the wall beside each chair. He fetched some water from the waterpot into the jug and set it with cups on each stool. Lazarus offered prayers after the food was served. Silence enveloped them as everyone was deep in thought. They mask the fear of losing each other; a thought none wanted after the loss of their parent at close intervals.

Mary remembered that night in Simon's house, the night the Lord brought peace to her troubled soul. Martha met the Lord as He was passing through Bethany. He was with a crowd of sick people asking for healing and miracles that He had done in other places. Martha had stayed and watched as the Saviour spoke with authority. He told the crowd to desire the healing of their souls and not only the healing of their bodies. He spoke about the Kingdom of His father which was coming soon and will replace all the kingdoms of men. Only those who come through the Son would be able to enter that Kingdom. Martha dropped her water pot and joined those who went before Him to be prayed for as they become a part of His Father's Kingdom.

Martha said that He lay hands on everyone who came out and when it was her turn, she felt a peace she had never felt before. It was like a mighty ocean cleaned and washed away all the sins, evil thoughts and deeds she had ever committed. She stood up and felt like a newborn baby. Her face glowed and her eyes sparkled, her laughter was infectious. From that time on, she became one of the followers of Christ. She would call Mary and speak to her about the need to amend her ways. Mary would listen to her and wish she knew how Martha had become transformed.

One afternoon, Mary and Lazarus delivered some goods to Edrago, a wealthy philistine in Adara village. Edrago was one of their father's biggest customers. Lazarus rode the colt while Mary sat on the cart with the goods. When they entered the vast compound, Edrago was not in but his three sons were. In the compound was an altar for their god, Dagon. The smell of incense wafted on them and one of the sons sprinkled a liquid on them. Mary shook off this liquid with her scarf as her head was fully covered. Lazarus was friends with the sons and they talked for some time, while Mary waited. Lazarus would leave Mary in the cart sometimes and go into their house. He always returns with one or two wineskins. He would drink a little and keep the rest, charging Mary never to tell anyone.

This day was no different. The compound looked deserted. Only the sons were in to collect and pay for the goods. After delivery, Lazarus went in with the eldest son to get the money. One of the other sons came close and tried talking to her but she refused to reply to him. He reached for her scarf and she slapped his hands away. This made him excited as he shouted and tried reaching for her again.

'Lazarus!' Mary called her brother, but there was no response.

At this point, she saw the eldest son coming out of the house without Lazarus.

'Where is Lazarus?' She asked and jumped down from the cart.

'Where is my brother, you infidel?'

As she moved towards the store, one of the brothers grabbed her from behind and lifted her off the floor. She screamed but it was too late. He gag her mouth with her scarf and carried her into a room. As she struggled, she saw Lazarus on the floor covered in blood with a skin of wine in his hand. She was defiled by the three brothers and no one came to her rescue.

When it became dark, they were dumped on the outskirts of the village. Lazarus woke up and became angry at the sight of his sister. They rode home in tears. Their father in fury, gathered men with Lazarus to demand justice for Mary. They razed down Edrago's house and his sons ran away.

The men of Edrago's village also joined forces to defend their own despite knowing the crime his sons committed. Ten men on both sides lost their lives and many were injured. Cyrus, Lazarus's father, was heavily wounded and he never recovered.

Mary stayed indoors for months as she could not bear being pointed at by people. Lazarus resorted to drink. Martha and their mother were mostly engrossed with taking care of Cyrus before he died. They also managed the business to raise money for his treatment.

Mary became withdrawn and reclusive. She would stay up all night crying and cursing. She started having violent nightmares about being defiled. It was a torture and she sometimes stayed awake to avoid the nightmares.

Whenever the ordeal was on, Martha and Lazarus would bang at her door. When they tried to restrain her, she threw them off with great strength. She would then beat and injure them severely. Since then, Martha had learned not to enter her room but rather stay at the entrance and pray for her. Anytime she prayed, Mary became relieved and would sleep deeply.

She began to desire men; their touch and violence. It seemed like demons had been deposited in her and her desire for men grew more each day. One night, she visited Racab, the harlot. Racab asked Mary what she wanted and she screamed men. The harlot gave her a strong drink and took her to a room. That night, four men came into her. She left the next morning after Racab paid her.

This became her life. She lost count of the men she slept with. She became rich but the wealth meant nothing to her. She bought jewellery and expensive spikenard oils with the money she made each night. As the money grew, so did the demons and the howling voices in her head. Sometimes, she would not sleep for days and would need a strong drink to finally get some sleep.

After Cyrus' death, their mother fell ill and died. Martha drew closer to the brethren and became a devoted believer. She tried bringing the Master to lay hands on their mother but the disciples told her the Master was busy. It can only be done if she brings her mother to Him. But she died before that could be done. Her death brought Him to their house. He comforted the family and prayed for Martha as Mary and Lazarus had gone out.

Martha never stopped urging Mary to meet the Master. Mary would laugh and decline. Simon, the leper who had been healed, invited the Master to his house on one of His visits to Bethany. Martha attended with Mary and Lazarus, and Simon gave them a good place at the table. Lazarus had too much to drink. He shuffled between the dance floor and the table.

The Master sat close to Simon and some of the disciples. He exuded so much peace amid the frenzy of music, food and drinks. When the musicians took a break to recoup, Lazarus danced back to the table.

'Lazarus, I am the Way, the Truth and Life, no one comes to the Father but by me.' Jesus says.

'Master, the burden of my sins is too heavy for anyone to carry. Pray for me in Your mercy that this weight will stop to assail my damned soul.'

He said playfully, looking at Mary who was curled in a corner and wrapped in a shawl. Her face was covered but he knew it was her from the smell of her spikenard oil. She had three different ones on her tonight; one from Ethiopia, Persia and Egypt. Using spikenard had become an obsession for her since the unfortunate incident. He could not even dare to think about it. He shuddered, not from taking too much wine, but from the piercing words that came from the master.

'Come to Me, all you that labour and are heavy laden and I will give you rest. For My yoke is easy and My burden is light.'

Just then, he saw Mary come towards the master and kneel at His feet. She kissed His feet and tears dropped. She wiped it with her hair that was now uncovered. From under her belt came a small jar of spikenard. She poured it on His feet and wiped it with her hair. The whole room was filled with the warm fondling aroma of the expensive spikenard. Judas, one of the disciples, condemned her but the Master rebuked him and blessed Mary.

At home, her heaviness suddenly disappeared. Her skin glowed, and she burst into a fit of laughter which continued all through the night. Lazarus couldn't sleep as the Master's voice kept ringing in His head through the rest of the night. As Mary laughed; he groaned. The effect of the wine disappeared.

At twilight, he waited for the Master at the North gate out of Bethany. Lazarus uncovered his face and knelt on His path. When the Master saw him, He laid hands on his head and whispered;

'Your sins are forgiven. Whoever the Son sets free is free indeed.'

He stayed silent for a while with His hands on Lazarus's head.

'Go in peace' He said and His train moved on. That was the moment Lazarus felt free and was indeed free from the anguish of guilt that had assailed him for years.

And now, Mary looked at Lazarus who had died after a brief illness, just like their mother. Lazarus had died but the Master brought him back to life. After the Master had been crucified, resurrected and ascended before many witnesses, Lazarus had become a strong witness, telling everyone what Christ could do for them. The chief priest had warned Lazarus to stop spreading falsehood. When Lazarus did not stop, he started sending bands of troublesome youths to their house to cause a commotion.

The three sharp knocks on the door were the sign of a friend. However, Martha would check through the crack in the door before opening it. She opened it to let in two men.

'It's John and Barnabas,' she announced as the two came in. They uncovered their heads and washed their feet in the bowls at the foot of the stone bench. They hugged and kissed Lazarus. Mary bowed slightly in greeting and they acknowledged the greeting as they took their seats. Mary and Martha brought water with a dish of nuts for the men and sat close to them.

'Brother Lazarus, you need to leave Bethany before morning.' John spoke first. 'The high priest and the council have planned with some youths, to forcefully stop you from talking about the Messiah. A plan is on to cause a riot. You and your sisters are no longer safe here. You have to leave', he continued.

John had friends among the followers of the high priest who were more loyal to him than to the high priest.

'These youths are dangerous sects under an oath to do the bidding of the council even if it meant death. They complain that many are turning to Christ because of your story.' Barnabas explained.

'My testimony is true. No one can do anything against the truth. Let them kill me, I am not afraid of them. I am only afraid for my sisters and our father's business. If not, I go nowhere. I fear only the one who can kill both the body and the spirit.'

Lazarus replied as he looked towards his sisters who were huddled in a corner listening to the men.

'Brother Lazarus, your death does not profit the Kingdom of Yahweh. He has given you a testimony that will bring more to the knowledge of His dear Son and our saviour. This testimony can be taken to another place, where many can hear and glorify the Father.' Barnabas, a disciple well-respected by many, spoke.

'But to where? Who will take care of Mary and Martha?'

'They are safe with the brethren. You can be sure of that. Cyprus is a place we are sure you will be safe in. The brethren there will take you in', John explained.

Just then, there was a bang on the door. It was Goke, a friend of Lazarus from Ibadan, the lower part of Ethiopia. He was tall and muscular, a royal prince who had come to Jerusalem on pilgrimage. He heard the story of Lazarus and Jesus, believed it and became a trusted friend.

He was now a trader of spices and a resident in Bethany. He had asked Lazarus to go away with him to his country, far from the threats of the high priest. Lazarus had declined and Goke had promised to stay by him through thick and thin. He banged on the door again.

'They are coming! The trumpet has sounded from the high priest's quarters.' Goke shouted. The party moved quickly and, in a rush, Lazarus was out of the house through the back door and into the bush behind the estate.

Three years later, a big event was to take place in Cyprus. Lazarus, who had moved to Kition, stood in front of a large crowd in the massive building that was built in two years. He was arrayed in purple robes, and not too far away, were Mary and Martha, both dressed in white apparel. They looked in awe at what God had done through Lazarus at Kition.

John, the Beloved was with Brother Paul and Barnabas to pray for Lazarus as the Bishop of Kition. Paul and Barnabas were on a missionary journey and had heard of the great work the Lord was doing through Lazarus and the brethren. They had taken a detour to strengthen the brethren. When they saw the great work being done by the Lord, they decided to stay longer to witness the dedication of the church building, and as led by the Holy Spirit, to pray for Lazarus who came to Kition three years earlier. Kition was a city in Cyprus.

When Lazarus arrived in Kition three years ago, the brethren loved him and took him in. He started visiting the city centre after a few days to speak about the love of Christ. Lazarus used witnessing and his gift of singing to bring many to Christ. The miracle of healing also drew crowds to him each night. Being filled with the Holy Spirit and wisdom, he was able to convert a leader at the city gate to the way of Christ. This man told many about Lazarus after being healed. Leaders and influential individuals invite him to their homes at night. Many of them got saved and healed. During the day, the crowds did not cease to seek him out too.

The word grew and the company of the brethren also enlarged. In a short time, the brethren, under the leadership of Lazarus secured a piece of land and began to build a sanctuary of worship.

At the sound of the horns and trumpet, Lazarus rose as motioned to by Paul, Barnabas and John, the beloved. He knelt and rested his hands on the bent knee. John the Beloved removed the cap at the back of his head. Paul poured oil on his head and the trumpet sounded again. Paul laid hands on Lazarus and the other two men followed suit as they began to speak in a heavenly language. Lazarus was prayed for as the first Bishop of Kition.

WHITE RIBBON

Death in Church

I thought being a pastor was the easiest job in the world. Since I was young, I had always seen pastors enjoy attention, honour and respect. They have nice houses, ride the best cars, wear expensive clothes and have beautiful wives. As I sat at the police station waiting for the divisional police officer, I remembered taking huge plates of food to the pastor's house every Christmas morning as a child. When I grew older, the pastors became younger, with nice cars and beautiful wives. I then wanted to become a pastor because even women old enough to be their mothers respect them.

Somebody had committed suicide in the church and I was invited by the police to give a statement because I am the pastor. Now I know a pastor's job is not as easy as I thought; pastors deal with people, the most difficult creature of God. When there is trouble in marriage, no food for a family, a sick relative, or death; everyone goes to the pastor.

Being a pastor was not just a childhood fantasy, it was what I felt called to do. I gave my life to Christ in the university after a 'Youth Aflame' crusade by a non-denominational Christian outfit for fresh students. We were counselled and handed over to the university fellowship. I became the fellowship president in my penultimate year after two years of great zeal and commitment. I was able to combine fellowship activities with the difficulty of the final year and graduated with a first-class degree.

My one year of the National Youth Service Corps programme went by so fast at the state chapter of the Nigerian Christian Corpers' Fellowship in Enugu where I served as the prayer secretary. When everyone went in search of a job, I felt called to ministry. After counselling with Pastor Kole Arija, a young pastor with a fast-growing ministry in town, I was sent to a Bible College and served in His ministry afterwards.

Two years later, He prayed for me and released me to fulfil my purpose. His ministry gave us all the support needed to start. The location was at Agbowo, close to the University of Ibadan. In a short while, we became the fastest-growing church in the city. The youth and upwardly mobile folks in the city found a place to worship and serve. I got married to a petite God-loving sister; Omolola and the work continued.

Within eight years, we've had three satellite centres and the church headquarters had started building a structure in the high-end area of Samonda. I was in my early thirties, with two adorable daughters, aged two years and nine months. All was going well with the work and being a pastor was rewarding, although there were few challenges. The ministry was a walk of faith.

I refused to give the junior police officers my statement until I see my lawyer and the DPO. The investigating officer informed me that the DPO was in a meeting with the area commander in the commissioner of police's office at the force headquarters. The voice of the IPO jolted me to reality.

'Pastor, the DPO is around now. If you are ready, he will see you or do you still want to wait for your lawyer?'

'Thank you, officer. I will see the DPO but will not make any statement until my lawyer gets here.'

He sounded nice unlike when we had a heated argument earlier concerning my refusal to give a statement. He had sent my assistants out, telling them that I was the one who had a case to answer.

I followed him to the DPO's office, which was well furnished, unlike the IPO and DCO's offices. The DPO was a well-dressed young man in his late thirties. He was a graduate and was well behaved too. I remember meeting him at a programme with the state commissioner for religious affairs. We exchanged pleasantries as I sat. He apologised for keeping me waiting and asked if I wanted water which I declined.

'What happened pastor?' He asked.

'One of our members committed suicide in the church. She was found dead this morning by a janitor who came to open the door for the cleaners.'

'Where is the janitor?'

'He is with your men, giving his statement.' I told him.

'Oh, nice. You need to give yours too', he said, drinking water from a glass cup placed on a flowery tray. His walkie-talkie was buzzing with updates from his men on the field.

'But why me DPO? The suicide note was found on her and it explained why the act was committed. This is a difficult time for the church,' I explained.

'I know pastor, this is standard procedure. I assure you of our cooperation and you will not be detained. We just need your statement as the head of the church. I have been briefed and have seen the suicide note.' He replied.

I simply nodded.

'What about the fiancé of the deceased?' he inquired.

'He is in the hospital. He collapsed on hearing the news', I replied.

'We would like to have a statement from him when he gets better.'

True to his words, I was not detained. After giving my statement in the presence of my lawyer, I was released and was to report the next day. The media went agog that night with the news of a female member who committed suicide in the church in her wedding dress.

The church board was called in for an emergency meeting. My wife with some elders visited the family of the deceased. The board agreed that a press statement is issued and I should hold a press conference to give the church's side of the story. My phone kept buzzing with calls. By the time I walked into my house a few minutes past midnight, I had concluded that a pastor's world was not as glamorous as I had thought as a child.

I was seated in the church conference room by eight the next morning for the press conference and interview. This was after the pastors' and workers' morning devotion. I was there with the assistant pastors and two church elders. We had met briefly after the prayers and we agreed on making our position known as a church than allow rumours and untruths to be peddled on the news and social media. Thirty minutes later, a press statement was drafted by Pastor Chris, a retired journalist who was in charge of media matters.

The suicide story became the headline of all local and some international media. There were different angles to the story and we were being labelled a church with ritual tendencies. Our quick rise, spread and success were now been questioned and analysed by many. Messages and calls flooded my phone. I ignored many but responded in monosyllables to respected leaders in the faith. Seeing that the press was all ready and stationed, I spoke to the microphone.

'Ladies and gentlemen of the press, can we have your attention please?'

The microphone was quickly adjusted to a lower decibel by the technical staff.

With deep shock, we received the death of our beloved Sis Agnes Ogene who committed suicide one week before her wedding. The circumstance of her action is already known to all of us as stated in the suicide note. As much as we believe that her reason for the act is shocking, it is not enough to justify such a painful act. We commiserate with her family, fiancé and the church. Knowing one's HIV/AIDS status is not a death sentence; we would have helped and supported her through the difficult time had we been informed. As a church, we stand only on Christ our solid rock, all insinuations of alliance with occultism are hereby denied and rejected in strong terms by the church. Thank you.

In ten minutes, I was done. I mentioned that we had nothing to fear and will cooperate with the police in their investigations. We were also working closely to support the family in the burial of the deceased. I stated that it is a challenging time for the church as every member is important and we would have loved to have things done differently. At this point, I asked if there were questions from the press. Many hands shot up. From a corner, I saw Pastor Chris shake his head but I ignored him. I saw him scribble something on his note pad which he passed to me.

'How close were you to the deceased?' A young reporter from the local private television station asked.

'As close as I am to every member of the church, but not as close as I am to some leaders because she was not a church leader'. I responded now, glancing at the note from Pastor Chris who counselled that I was not obliged to answer every question and to keep it as short as possible.

'Is this the first time a death such as this took place in this church?' A radio reporter asked after introducing himself.

'You are the media, do you have any news of such death before now?'

I fired back, trying to contain my anger. After putting myself together and praying under my breath for the help of the Holy Spirit, I continued; 'Death is a common factor to all mankind, while we have older people dying in church; they were mainly parents of members since we are a church populated with young people. Sister Agnes' death is the first and is most shocking.'

'Why suicide? Did the church push her into this by her policy?' Another piercing question hit me like a dart.

'Let me explain the policy of the church about marriage and wedding planning to you. Every intending couple is expected to notify their leaders of their marriage plans after conviction from God. The leaders will join them in prayers and if they also receive confirmation from God, they will be referred to the marriage committee. The committee will interview and refer them for counselling. A notice of six months is usually requested by the church for adequate planning and support. Before the wedding ceremony, certain tests are conducted including HIV/AIDS status tests. '

I stopped to catch my breath and then continued.

'It was at this point that Sister Agnes discovered that she was HIV positive and decided to end it all. From her suicide note, you will note that she was a rape victim and must have contacted it from that horrible experience. We feel ending it with suicide was not the best solution, we could have counselled and guided her through with full support. Every life is a gift from God and must be held in sanctity. I guess she was afraid of possible rejection by her husband-to-be, his family and probably society.'

'There are rumours that her death may not be a suicide case but maybe ...', the short lady in a pink dress with heavy make-up said, finishing the sentence with a gesticulation that left the conclusion to the imagination.

'If you or anyone have proof that her death is beyond suicide, please feel free to assist the police in their investigations. The scripture says that the righteous are as bold as a lion. We are not afraid.'

Pastor Chris came to my rescue. 'I am sure the pastor has been kind enough to take some of your questions. Other questions can be directed to the church phone number that will be given to those who do not have it and I can assure you that you will get an appropriate response.'

'Finally, the church will be setting up a foundation in memory of our late sister to offer advisory services and other support to people living with HIV and AIDS. There will be counselling, provision of drugs and support for this group of people. We will also set up protocols that will help reduce, and ultimately, eradicate stigmatisation against people living with the virus.'

I said this and looked at the press with confidence. I saw a few of them nodding in acceptance. The last statement was not planned but I felt it was the prompting of the Holy Spirit.

The weeks that followed were hectic as the burial of Sister Agnes took centre stage and the church had to heal. A foundation was set up to provide advisory and counselling support for people living with HIV and AIDS or their relations. My wife and I felt led to be the vanguard of the work and offered to be available for counselling and support. An office was set up and funding was provided.

Three months after, activities started in earnest and I got my first counselling appointment. It was with Mama Jacinta, a restaurant owner, not far from the church. Her restaurant specialises in delicacies from the eastern part of the country. She had attended our services a few times at the invitation of her son, Calister Junior, popularly called Brother CJ who is a member of the choir.

Mama Jacinta

Wednesdays are for my counselling appointments. Information had gone out that other pastors and I were available for counselling. It was a wet afternoon after lunch hour. The air-conditioner in the office was on fan mode. It was cold but bearable.

Dola, my secretary, ushered Mama Jacinta into the office and brought her to my desk. She was a light-complexioned woman in her early fifties, plump and buxomly. She must have been slim and striking beauty in her youth but age had added flesh and cares to a now not-too-fair complexion. She was dressed in an Ankara blouse and wrapper with the matching piece as a scarf.

'Good afternoon, pastor. Thank you for seeing me. Do you remember me?' she asked.

'Good afternoon, Madam. Yes, I do. CJ's mother?' I replied and she cut in quickly.

'Please CJ is not aware I am here' she said pleading for anonymity.

'No problem, Madam. You are safe with us.'

'It is Baba Jacinta. He is sick and what he told me, I need to share it with you so that you can pray and help us too.'

She went straight to her story.

'I met Baba Jacinta when I had just finished secondary school and was helping my mother sell food. He also just left his boss who trained him in the transportation business. He was a driver for someone who owns a bus. They shared the bus for trips to Aba and travelled five days a week. He was always in our shop whenever he was off duty. He calls me "yellow pawpaw". He was kind, caring and had a good sense of humour. He brought gifts from his journeys for me. My mother and sisters loved him but my father did not. He wanted me to marry one of his drunkard friends who already had a harem.' She paused for breath.

'My father insisted that it was either his friend or no other person. I had no choice but to run away with Calister. I came back home heavily pregnant and Calister asked my father for his blessing so that I could be his wife properly. My father drove us away with a cutlass, calling him a kidnapper. He was arrested by the police but later released after intervention by family members. My father never gave his consent until he died but Calister never stopped performing his duties as a son-in-law.'

She continued as I listened intently.

'Calister prospered in his business after our second child, Calister Junior was born. I was now in the restaurant business and doing well as a start-up. We agreed not to have more children to give the best to the two we have. They went to the schools our income could afford. After Jacinta's secondary school education, my sister in London offered to help her become a nurse. All the money we had saved up to buy land and build a house was used for her schooling in London. Thank God, she is now a nurse.'

'About this time, my husband's behaviour changed. He would spend weeks on a trip and blame it on faulty vehicles. He now owned three buses; two were being used by employed drivers. He stopped giving us money for feeding and was not interested in paying CJ's school fees. I did my best to fulfil the responsibilities he had neglected. He stopped his marital obligations to me and abandoned our bed.'

'Our elders say there is no smoke without fire. He had never had any other woman just like I had never known any other man before our marriage.' She wiped the tears from her eyes with the headgear that she removed.

'Things went down for his business and he sold the buses one after the other. He stopped going to work, stayed at home all day and go out at night to drink. One day, I came home and met a woman with two sons at our doorstep. The boys were ten and twelve years old. They were exact replicas of my husband and younger versions of CJ. He took them away and when he came back, we had a real fight after twenty-three years of marriage.'

'I felt betrayed and stopped talking to him and feeding him. News also got to me about a prostitute my husband stayed with on days he was not home. I stopped giving him money. When he had no money to throw around, the "ashawo" threw him out and moved to another idiot.'

'This is my life's story, pastor. My husband is badly emaciated and has an annoying cough. He has begged me to forgive him but what is there to forgive? I want you to meet and speak with him. I don't want him to die even though I don't love him again. I suspect a strange disease. Maybe you can help.'

I thanked Mama Jacinta for coming and promised to take up her case. We visited him and offered to help him through our medical outreach programme. He accepted and over time, he was diagnosed to be HIV positive. He confessed that he had known from an earlier report but was afraid of telling his wife. We encouraged her to take the test and she tested negative. Even though the family was devastated, the church supported them with care and counselling.

Gladys

My second guest was also a woman, a member of the church. She was a single mother of two. She had insisted on seeing me instead of my wife. When asked about a joint meeting with both of us, she agreed but my wife had to attend to our daughter who was down with a cold. So here I was with Sis Gladys Obaro. Her look had changed recently. She worked as a junior-level marketing and sales officer at one of the micro-finance banks in town. Though very busy with her job and kids, she tried to be available in church as time permits.

She sat before me distraught and you could tell that she had endured sleepless nights and sobbing bouts. She was dressed in a cream blouse and a jeans skirt. She used her scarf to wrap her head in the Arabian style and hid her swollen eyes behind dark glasses, which she has now removed.

'I am in a mess pastor,' she began.

'Work or home?' I inquired as I know the stories of how risky the banking industry was, especially for a woman with a family.

'Home pastor, big time. My labours are in vain. I am in deep trouble. Where do I start from pastor?'

'Calm down sister, please start from somewhere. There is nothing bigger than God or too difficult for Him to handle.'

I tried to calm her down while giving her a paper handkerchief to dry her tears.

'Bombings by Boko Haram terrorists in Abuja which killed my husband's uncle and boss drove us to Ibadan. I had just had a baby, so we decided I should stay at home to nurse the baby. Efe, my husband agreed to his friend's invitation and we moved in with him in a three-bedroom flat at Orogun. Jerry's wife was in the USA and plans were on for him to join her there. He said it would be cost-effective for us to live together and possibly take over the house when he was gone. He also said he uses only one room and a woman in the house would solve all his culinary shortfalls.'

She paused.

'Jerry was such a nice man. He fed us with his income while Efe was trying to secure a job in the new environment. Jerry's papers finally pulled through. He left everything in the flat for us, paid for the next year's rent and drop some cash to support us. Settling down in the US was not easy for Jerry. He had to take some courses before he could get a job and had to rely on his wife's income to solve a myriad of financial commitments. Our source of support was, therefore, cut off after Jerry left. Efe refused to take low-paying jobs out of pride and we were losing weight because of poor diet while barely trying to keep the child well fed. I then got pregnant again!' She sighed.

I offered her water now. She seeped a little and wiped the tears from her face with the paper handkerchief.

'He asked me to abort the pregnancy but I refused. Since I was good at making hair which I had learnt from my mother who was a hair stylist, I joined a big saloon two streets away from home to earn a living. He was too proud to take a low-paying job compared to when he was a production manager in Abuja. I pushed myself despite the pregnancy and my two-year-old daughter, to go to work every day. The job was helping us to meet basic needs at home. He agreed to babysit our daughter while I worked and he spent every other time in front of the computer. He came up with stories of how Jerry was settling down and working out something for us. That brought a ray of hope.'

'Thank God' I interjected.

'Two months after the birth of the second baby I had to resume work at the salon because my husband was still not working. His friends and family had supported us with hospital bills for the baby and the first month. It was at the salon that I met Sister Ayobami who brought me to church after she preached and I gave my life to Christ. She nurtured me as her disciple and helped me secure the banking job.'

'At first, Efe asked me not to take the job. He asked how I would cope with two children and a banking job. I begged him to help out while I get a maid because the banking job was going to give us four times what I was earning at the salon. He refused to budge. My mother came in to assist for two months before a maid was secured for us. She cautioned me to watch out for my husband; it was as if he was up to something. I asked if she caught him with another woman but she was not affirmative.'

Gladys started sobbing again. I tried to calm her down.

'I came home unexpectedly one day. Efe had gone out, so I ran through his things and found a file of documents. He had collected an international passport without my knowledge, secured a divorce from me and had married a white woman in Lagos three weeks earlier. The ground spun under me, I wished it could swallow me alive. I wanted to keep the file; I wanted to burn it all. I took pictures of it with my phone and hid the file away on the ceiling. I burned with anger. I thought of poisoning his food but stopped with the help of the Holy Spirit and Sister Ayobami. I kept quiet waiting for his reaction.'

'Three days later, he discovered the file was missing and eventually found it where I hid it. He begged me and said it was all for our good. He wanted to tell me everything after "his new wife" had helped him secure a visa to join her as the husband. I refused to believe him and called him a traitor. Since he was not coming to church with me, he got people to beg me and swore he would never neglect me and the children. He said he planned to use the marriage to get into the US, divorce her and bring us into the country. He said it was the fastest route to leave the country and become an American citizen'.

'After many appeals, I agreed. He suddenly changed, he became nice and started coming to church. He was fasting, praying and being nice at home. I fell for his scheming. Six months later, his papers came through and he left. That was the last I heard of Efe. Jerry, his friend, had also lost contact with him. I became a single mother.'

'I am aware of this part and we have been praying along for you, Sister Gladys.'

'Thank you, pastor.'

She continued, 'My job has been hectic and has resulted in less time with my children. I have become like a stranger to them. Mary, my maid, had almost become their mother. Two weeks ago, Tomi, my colleague, got a new maid. She was tested for HIV and Hepatitis B and the results were negative. Tomi said this was her usual practice because a maid had once tested positive for HIV. It was at this point I remembered I did not ask Mary to take any of such tests. She took the test that same weekend and came out positive for Hepatitis B. I was shocked. The virus is contracted mostly through sexual activities I presume?'

I was not sure if she was asking or telling me.

'I am not sure too. We can get more information about it.' I replied, a matter of fact.

'I took my children for the test and they came out positive, pastor! Positive...' She almost screamed. 'What should I do? My husband is gone, and my children have a killer virus in their system. All my labour and toil, are they not in vain? This is too much for me.'

'Where do I go from here?'

She broke down on the floor in a kneeling position and started crying again. Just then, my wife came in to pick me up. She was my saving angel at this time as she took over.

After staying close to Gladys who developed suicidal tendencies, we discovered that Hepatitis B was not a killer disease. The children were not showing any signs and their health could be managed without any danger or threat to life. The maid was sent away after some medical interventions and Gladys' mum came to live with her. Gladys became more stable emotionally and more committed to the church. She has put in place a plan to exit the bank and switch to a career that would allow her to spend more time with her children.

I saw that the actual work of a pastor was the impact he or she would have on the people outside of preaching engagements. I promised myself to be more committed to being available to care for the people God has asked me to shepherd.

Kamo Dollar

My next counselee was not a member of the church. He was my childhood friend, brought back into my life by

God. My parents were retired civil servants. My mother retired as a primary school head teacher and my father worked till retirement in the ministry of lands and housing. They lived at College Crescent around the Oke-Ado area of the city. I have lunch with them fortnightly and usually go along with items on their shopping list.

One Friday afternoon, I was in the cocoa house mall to pick up items on their shopping list at Foodco supermarket when I noticed a man in black jeans, a light blue shirt and a Kangol cap staring at me. He was smiling as he moved closer. The relics of bleached skin were evident; he had a gold wrist watch and large rings on three fingers with a chain hanging visibly under his shirt collar. I was used to being approached by strangers because of our weekly programme on the local TV station. I smiled back but he kept moving toward me.

'Agba, Baba pastor, Omo Mama teacher. I salute you, Baba pastor.'

The man said as he got closer. This cannot be a total stranger as he knew my mother was a teacher. I tried to recollect the face but I couldn't.

'Have we met before?' I asked.

'Yes o, long time ago and I also dey see you for television and tell my people say your mother na my papa customer.'

'Ehn, oh that is nice. And you are ...?' I asked.

'Me? I be Kamoru Yussuf, Omo baba eleran, the meat seller; Fuji musician AKA Kamo Dollar', he smiled as he thrust his hand forward. I stretched both hands forward to show it was filled with items and a shopping basket.

'No problem' he smiled back.

'Sorry, I did not remember your face. I remember Baba Kamo very well. He was my mother's meat seller for many years till she retired. We both have left home a long time ago. So how are you?'

'Baba, life tough o. Things no easy o. KD just dey survive', He replied.

I was wondering why somebody about my age could be calling me "Baba" which means father and is usually meant for older people. I know pastors and spiritual leaders are usually accorded this fatherly role and respect. I noticed Kamo Dollar's bloodshot eyes and dark lips, the signature of a serial cigarette smoker.

'Christ gives us peace from all troubles if we come to Him' I quickly quipped.

He just shrugged. I felt he had something in his mind that he would like to offload. I brought out my appointment call card after dropping the basket on the floor and gave him one.

'If you know our church at Samonda, you could come to see me on Wednesday next week at three in the afternoon so we can talk more. How is Baba Kamo now?' I asked.

'He is fine o but na market Baba dey stay now. Baba Kamo na leader of meat sellers at Oje and Bere. Mama teacher nko; how she dey?' He weaves in and out of pidgin English.

'I am on my way to see her. I will tell her I saw you. Please, see you next week.'

We turned in different directions and I could hear him hum a tune as he walked on, tucking the card into his pocket.

Kamo Dollar was at the church fifteen minutes before his appointment and was offered snacks and a beverage drink. When he walked into the office at the exact time of our appointment, he hailed me.

'Baba pastor, always on time. Respect!' he said with much enthusiasm.

He goes on to sing a skit in Fuji, hailing my promptness, humility and care for others. I watched in admiration of his talent. He indeed had a good voice that sounded tired and wearied by alcohol and cigarette.

'Please sit down KD, you are welcome to my office and how are you today?' I asked as I surveyed him. He was dressed in an Ankara shirt and trousers with his trademark Kangol cap. As usual, his neck and fingers were decked with costume neck chains and rings. His eyes today were hidden behind dark glasses.

'Thank you, Baba', he said as we sat at my guest sitting area, away from my desk.

'So, how is your family and how is Fuji music? I am not a fan but I have heard about you in the news. What is happening to you now?'

'Baba, things no de easy. Things no dey like this before. When money dey, many many friends dey but when money grow wings; friends go fly away. That is life, Baba.'

'Tell me what happened.' I inquired.

'It is Baba God that gave me a good voice to sing every time, I like to sing, compose a song from anything. If I see an ant on the floor, I go compose song for am. My friends and I dey sing for the Muslim fasting month and at festivities. One year during the Ileya festival, some people organised a competition for us at Bere. Me, I beat all of them from Bere to Oje and Gate area. Radio people come there and so, they took me to a radio station where one promoter like me and say make we work together. That na how we go studio to record with my friends after dem give us instruments and we sign papers. Our band that time na 'Youngsters Fuji band'. Our beat dey fast and people fit dance well well to the music, unlike dem old musicians.'

He took a sip from his drink and wiped the sweat from his brows. I wondered why he was sweating under the air-conditioner.

'Young people like us well well and we dey everywhere for Ibadan, Abeokuta, Osogbo. One day after one show for Yemetu, one man called Balo, his real name na Yusuf Balogun come to me that, I fit do well on my own and that he go help me as my manager if I leave the band. He take me to see some promoters and one record company wey promised me many things. After our contract with the former promoter ended, I follow Yusuf Balogun.'

'Balo became my manager, that na wetin we dey call am. I dey with him with some other young musicians. He rented a house for us and bought two cars with drivers for all of us to share. He dey collect money from our shows and give us part of it. Life dey good for all of us young artists. Money, booze, hemp and women dey flow around us.' He paused for breath.

'Baba, you will know Leke; gospel Fuji?'

I nodded in affirmation. Leke, known as Lakeside is a renowned gospel artist in the city of Ibadan who is versatile with a tinge of Fuji music as a blend to his style of gospel music.

'We dey together under Balo, he dey very young then. We used to call am 'small boy' but he left one day, he say he wan play gospel music. Balo asked him why and he said he don become born again. All of us dey laugh him but Balo allowed him to go. Balo no give am any money from the pool, he say the money na for us not for mister born again. Then, I came up with one record wey the title be "*Dollar Fuji*". That record na in come hit well well; everybody dey dance to my *Dollar Fuji*.'

He stood up and demonstrated the dance steps that caught on like wildfire among the youths years back.

'So it was you? You must have made a lot of money from that album.'

'I make am o Baba. I bought a house at Bashorun with two cars. Balo no keep my money again o. I don get sense, I get my banker wey be account officer; bastard girl wey dey always wear short short skirt.'

I shook my head at his cursing. He apologised and continued.

'We signed a contract and na only twenty-five percent of anything I make e dey get. Within two years, three women don born children for me. Mama Kamo, my mother, who don dey go church say God no like this kind life. She say make I marry one of them and be sending money to take care of the others. You know say no child be bastard sha.'

He was on his feet now, gesticulating as he spoke.

'Na Silifa I chose wey fine pass them the other two. Silifa na African queen. Na there I get am wrong. Silifa dey smoke weed, drink and dey do white powder too. I want the baddest beautiful woman for my side. Silifa na witch and daughter of the devil and hell. We go everywhere; Ghana, London and Lagos, huge fan clubs dey there too. Kamo Dollar as dem call me now, the son of a meat seller, the thing enter my head too much. Drinking, smoking and 'Casi' that na Casino, we dey do everywhere. As money dey come na so e dey go. Money na visitor, if you no take care of money, e go go another person house o.'

He continued, 'Silifa fit fight anywhere, especially with my female fans who want to get close. Two albums after *Dollar Fuji* no sell well. Another one come and struggle for market. But Baba, nothing like *Dollar Fuji*. One of my fans come take me to see one Baba herbalist wey go do ritual for me to make my music sell well well and fame go come get bigger and go everywhere. That one we dey call ww.fame wey mean worldwide fame. Na woman we go use, either my wife or my mother for the ritual. Baba, many musicians dey do this ritual to blow and get more name but e dey get bad bad side effects sha. I no dey ready to use my mother; Mama Kamo. Silifa na the option, wallahi. I agree to use her. Nothing spoil, na ogbanje and witch she be before.'

He continued, 'Na isolation for seven days I go stay, then Silifa go visit me and she will be used.' He was silent for a few minutes. His voice cracked with emotions.

'Na my paddy wey be my fan nah in sell me. Bastard, I no know say he dey sleep with Silifa. She don jazz this guy, na anything he go do for Silifa o. He get money and he dey sell drugs too. He fit kill him mama for Silifa sef. The whole plan come leak to her and she leak am to the newspaper people, radio o, television o. Everybody just dey carry the news. She run follow the man go America with my daughter. I never see them since then o.' He wiped away a tear.

He continued, 'I can never have children again o, Baba pastor. The taboo for ritual na if Silifa no come, I go run mad or never get children again. Baba herbalist do some rituals make I no run mad but go never get children again o'. He was sobbing seriously now.

After some time, he became calm and started talking again.

'Nobody wan touch Kamo Dollar again because of bad news. I go into hiding and only came out to do small show for the low side of the city where I come from; Bere and Oje. For that side, laye ... I was still big boy o and homeboy to these ones. Iya won... You know Bere and Oje na the drug place for Ibadan. I move from Casinos to betting and drugs.'

'One day, we dey betting games like that, na him fight come start and one boy come stab me and run away. Na for the hospital dem come know say I dey do drugs.'

He was quiet now. I respected the emotional journey recap and said nothing. He continued.

'After many many months, I no dey take coke again but only weed dey around me. I sell many things to live. No woman go stay with a man who wan offer his wife for sacrifice. Prostitutes come and go, only the baddest ones among them fit stay for a while. I don spend all my life to be successful in music. I no go school and never do business or trade. Three years wey person no get good album wey blow, e no go dey easy like that. Now, na saje and street language with tech beats dem dey use. Me no get home, no wife, no money, no fame, alone I dey inside this terrible world.' He started sobbing.

I was at his side and tried to comfort him. I knew the void and gap could only be filled by one person; the Lord of hosts Himself-the Lord Jesus! We could not talk any longer that evening but we struck a strange friendship. I was bent on helping this man find his humanity again. I invited Lakeside to lunch with KD. They were both surprised to see each other after many years. The reality of what could happen to one who followed the path of righteousness and one who sought the pride of life was evident as both men sat opposite each other. Lakeside was now a successful gospel artist with a great and stable family. With Lakeside, KD had someone to look up to and identify with. He started attending church and gave his life to Christ one afternoon while having lunch at Kokodome restaurant. Inside my car, Kamo Dollar confessed Christ with Lakeside watching.

Three months later, we launched the church outreach programme, code-named; OPERATION WHITE RIBBON. This was for the community borne out of the death of Agnes and members of the community where the church was located. I saw the whole essence of the church. The outreach was not just to our members who were holy on Sundays but are experiencing various challenges and problems bottled up but to everyone in need.

My ministry should be like that of the Master who went to seek out the people where they were and met their needs. He gave them bread and meat; both physical and spiritual. He looked past the foibles of his disciples and patiently moulded them while bearing their infirmities.

In the crowd was Mama Jacinta who was more radiant after being counselled to forgive her husband and hope for the best. He was now under the support system of the church and an NGO for people living with HIV/AIDS.

Gladys had quit her job after setting up a fashion designing outlet. She was also the head of the youth empowerment programme of the church and was working on a feasibility study with some members to set up a microfinance scheme for members and non-members of the church.

Kamo Dollar was seated beside his mentor, Lakeside, who was working with him on a collaborative track on Lakeside's upcoming album. I clutched my wife's left hand and squeezed it. The white ribbon on the lapel of everyone's dress was an emblem of the united commitment of all, to be a helping hand to someone in need in the church or the community.

'Agnes did not die in vain. Her death just woke us up to more work that needed to be done.' I whispered as I stood to declare the formal opening of the church's welfare and support programme.

TANGLED

TANGLED

The thick smell of antiseptics used in hospitals usually gets his stomach churning but after many months in and out of the University College Hospital in Ibadan, he was now indifferent to it. His father had said it was a thing of the mind. His mind raced back to yesterday which was the final meeting of the Nigeria Football Association supporters club who were privileged to be on the train to the World Cup in Russia.

The world cup was held every four years and after many political manoeuvring and concessions, Russia was the host of the 2018 World Cup in the summer. Participating countries had the opportunity of bringing fans and to boost tourism, visa restrictions were usually relaxed to encourage huge returns on investment in infrastructures for the host country.

Marcus had been able to secure tickets for six matches, including the finals at a high price. He had been playing for the football club of a tobacco company in Ibadan which was struggling to move to the second division of the National Football League. He's always had his eye on travelling to Europe to play in the professional leagues but has not had the opportunity for trials, despite being linked with an agent there. The agent asked him to relocate to Europe because it will be easier and less expensive to go for trials if he stays nearby. He applied for a British visa twice but was rejected both times. This world cup in Russia was the golden opportunity he wanted to explore.

Now, he was at the hospital to say goodbye to his mother who was hospitalized because of a kidney disease three weeks ago. She had been in and out of the hospital in the last two years. This had drained the family emotionally and financially. His father, who worked at the Central Bank of Nigeria as a supervisor to note-checking staff, had been under much pressure. Marcus' prayer was to settle down quickly in Europe and be able to bring his mother in for the best treatment in any of the developed countries. His mother's younger sister and another paid auxiliary staff were always with her. There was no way he could tell her or anyone, that he was going away for a football tournament. After much debate and argument, his father agreed to the journey and agreed to keep it a secret from his mother.

He stayed with his mother for two hours and he said goodbye to the two women taking care of her after handing them some cash. He had hired a cab that would take him to the airport in Lagos where he would join the other group of fans.

The cab driver was a calm young man in his thirties who was probably into the business out of unemployment. He steered the car towards Total Garden and through Yemetu to Beere. As they weaved through the ancient part of the city, he remembered his grandmother who died ten years ago. She stayed at Yemetu but sold fruits at Oje market. She was religious and would wake him up at five o'clock, take him and his cousin, who she usually hijacks to stay with her on holidays, to observe early morning prayers after the bell had been rung. Both would follow her sleepily and often get knocks on the head if they dozed off during prayers. By six o'clock, she was already at the market after leaving a dish of *Ogi* and *Akara* or *moinmoin* for the boys.

It was during his stay with her, while on holiday, that he discovered his love for soccer and passion for music. With a grandmother who attended church twice a day, there was no way a young man would not seek refuge and music was just it for him and his cousin. He started to look forward to the holidays with his grandmother because there was always lots of soccer and music with good food. No matter how much you got on her nerves, Mama Agba, as she was called by all, would punish you with prayers, although it may be accompanied with a knock, a pinch on the ear or a stroke of the cowhide.

'Folorunso, God will make you great'. Two knocks go to the head; ko..ko..ko. 'You see me making *Ogi* and you are playing football'. Another knock goes to the boy's head, held hostage by a firm grip on his shirt.

'Do you want to be Thunder Balogun or Pele?'

Mama Agba would pinch the boy's ear as he screams to get out of her tight grip. Mama Agba was a disciplinarian but loving at the same time. His father fuelled his love for music by sending him to music classes where he learnt some musical instruments back home. He was soon certified as a multi-talented instrumentalist which he used freely in his home church. As he grew older, football became an obsession and he did less music.

The rest of the trip to Lagos was quiet and brought back memories of his childhood. He was now in the midst of a crowd all decked in different sorts of sportswear that announced them as football fans on the way to Russia for the world cup. The music was loud and the dancing was a spectacle. Faces were painted in the green-white-green colour of the national flag. Different flights left that night for a sixteen hour trip to Russia.

While onboard, he dreamt of his grandmother. She brought a drum for him to play for the church but he held on to a football and shook his head in response. His grandmother wrenched the ball from him, threw it into the mouth of a wild dog, and threw the drum at him. The drum grew bigger, choking him as he screamed, trying to free himself. He woke up with a start. He checked the in-flight map to discover that they were flying past North Africa. The flight attendant was in his aisle, looking down at him with a smile.

'Please could you give me a glass of water?' Marcus asked. She nodded and moved away.

Malchus sat with his back to the wall. He heaved a sigh. His blood pumped faster as his heart skipped a beat. He always felt like this when Caiaphas the high priest send them to the street to dishevel the camp of the disciples of the one who called himself the Messiah. He bent down to strap up his leather sandal. His mother moved into the open yard and placed the pot of water from her shoulder on the clay stool at the corner.

She covered it with a tray. She fetched a clay cup from the tray on the wooden shelf hung on the wall and took water from the clay jug. She took a sip and sighed. The shawl around her neck was used to wipe her face. She glanced at the knife hanging from the belt strapped around Malchus's waist. Their eyes met as Malchus reached for the fitted coat and wore it to conceal the knife.

'What seems good to the high priest Caiaphas this day and time, hun?' She said as she sat not too far from her son.

'He blasphemes each day. He calls himself the Messiah. He says He is equal to Yahweh. He wants to destroy the temple and build it back in three days. What madness is this? This must stop, it must.' Malchus told his mother.

'What if all He claims are true?' She asked.

'No mother, it can never be true. A man claiming to be equal to Yahweh?'

'Don't be part of this son. No man fights for Yahweh, He fights for Himself', she said as she stood and held his hands. Her dream the previous night flashed through her mind and she shuddered. He took her hand and kissed it. He picked the shawl, draped it over his head and headed out.

After walking down two streets, he entered the chief priest's quarters and went to the high priest's home. A crowd of young men were already gathered. Caiaphas had requested for a band of soldiers who he paid to provide back-up for the motley crew. The group moved out as darkness was settling on the land. They were equipped with lanterns, torches, clubs, knives and other weapons. The crowd moved towards the Kidron River. Judas was leading them on for he knew the garden where the deceiver met with His disciples to pray. Judas was needed to point Him out as he was sometimes hardly recognized among His disciples.

As they entered the garden of Gethsemane, Judas led the way and the young men followed closely. The troops had been asked to stay at the rear and provide support if the young men could not arrest the Son of Man.

Nigeria was in group 'D' of the 2018 world cup in Russia with Argentina, Croatia and Iceland. He was billed to watch all the Nigerian matches as he had paid for it. The first match was to hold on the 16th of June. The fans stuck with the team throughout the training period and offered criticism which the coaching crew were finding very probing and annoying at the same time. Many of the fans were in Russia as an escape route out of Nigeria. Their focus was not on the matches but on how to slip into Europe through Russia's borders.

He met the football scouting agent, who was trying to get him into Finland, with some documents and he quickly organised some try-outs. If it clicked, he would go back to Nigeria and the club will bring him through a contract into Finland.

The first meeting with Dimitri went well and he was quite impressed with videos of his games with the club in the Nigeria football league. Dimitri said it was best to get him out to Helsinki, Finland before the final matches of Nigeria in the group stages because if Nigeria did not get past the group stages, the team could be asked to leave with the fans and the radar will be monitoring the national supporters club closely. Marcus agreed to the plan and on the night of the Nigeria match with Iceland, Marcus was smuggled out to Finland.

The try-out went on for a week and ended not as well as Marcus expected. He was asked to come back in six months for another try-out. Dimitri asked that they go back to St. Petersburg and promised to secure a visa for Marcus in six months. He said it would be easy since they had secured documents to show they had a try-out and had another invitation in six months.

'Okay. No problem my man. Six months, you come back and we will get into this club. I promise you.' Dimitri said, trying to reassure Marcus.

But Marcus was sceptical. Most of the discussions were done in Finnish which he could not understand. He thought about the one thousand dollars fee he paid Dimitri to organise the soccer try-out with the Finnish club. Where would he get such money coupled with flight tickets and other expenses in six months? He simply nodded.

'No problem, Dimitri' He replied.

They went for lunch at a restaurant on the street. While Dimitri was gulping the meal at Marcus's expense, Marcus was plotting another game. Towards the end of the meal, Marcus stood up.

'Gents', he simply said.

Dimitri stared at him trying to comprehend. He simply gesticulated and he understood. Marcus went with his backpack. In the toilet, he locked himself in a cubicle and changed into another sports trunk and a hoddie which he pulled up. He brought out his purse and its contents, distributing them into the many pockets of his shirts. He dumped the bag into the waste bin at the entrance and walked out through another door. He glanced over his shoulders and saw Dimitri still gulping down the glass of alcohol. He crossed the street, brought out his map and walked away from his Russian friend into the arms of a newfound friend or foe; Helsinki.

'Malchus, wait, Malchus! Hold on.'

Jonah called after his friend who was running frantically toward home. Malchus looked back when he couldn't hear the call again. Jonah had stopped. He must have turned back. The plot was thickening. No one knew it would be so easy to arrest the man who called Himself a Messiah. He touched the ear again. It was still there; it was intact and not dangling. It was in place but the blood around it had caked up on his neck and was a grim reminder of the incident.

He got home, opened the wooden door, entered and latched the lock. His mother came into the passageway still holding the cloth she was folding after washing. She saw the blood stain on his cloth and as she moved closer, she saw a trail on his neck.

'What happened?' she asked.

There was silence. The look on her face showed that there was no getting away from answering the question. He touched the ear again.

'Peter drew the sword and cut my ear', he simply said as if it did not matter.

He went to the earthen pot in the corner, took the bowl on it, and scooped some water. He poured the water into a cup from the wooden tray and drank it. Before his mother could talk, he stammered and continued.

'Jesus put it back. Can you believe that? I can't believe this man is what He says He is. Son of God? Absolutely not! Joseph was his father and Mary his mother. He must have gained the power from a demon' Malchus said.

'Have you seen any demon do what he did?' His mother asked.

Malchus just shrugged.

'My son, you cannot kick against the stones. He has shown you that He is not a deceiver. Stop chasing a lie. Could Caiaphas have healed you or restored the ear that was cut off? Son, stop this madness with the high priest. Have you thought about why it was you that was hurt? Yahweh is calling your attention. Heed, heed, today.' She shook her fist at him.

'Are you one of His disciples too?'

'I wish I was and you too' She mumbled under her breath. She did become one after a few days but not him.

Marcus turned on the two-by-six feet bed. He rubbed his face and yawned, his muscles ached and desired more sleep. The occupant of the other bed had snored through the night which did not give him much chance at a sound sleep since he was a light sleeper. He had about two hours of deep sleep. The buzzer from the alarm that served as a chapel bell in the shelter home sounded again. It was an invitation for morning prayers.

This was his second month at the shelter for homeless people. After he ran away from Dimitri, he mixed into the market crowd and found a place in the park which was occupied by tourists from different races. He sent a WhatsApp message to his friend, Kole, in Nigeria about his experience.

Marcus: Oh boy, I don japa!

Kole: My guy, that is Naija sense. Where are you?

Marcus: In a park with a large crowd of tourists.

Kole: Great. What next?

Marcus: Thinking and calculating.

Kole: Be focused, relax and don't act edgy. Buy a drink, if you have a camera, start taking pictures.

Marcus: You are a genius.

Kole: If you have a map, look around you for a shelter or google it if you are finding it difficult on the map.

Marcus: Shelter?

Kole: They offer free accommodation and support to immigrants.

True to Kole's words, the shelter proved secure. He had been there for months now. The shelter was run by a seventy-year-old American missionary, Pastor Cole Briggs, who preferred to be called Brother Cole or simply Cole. Brother Cole had been in Finland for fifteen years and had run the shelter. He initially came to Finland on holiday with other missionaries but fell in love with the country and its people. He went back home to Chicago to arrange a final journey to Helsinki and had been there since. Brother Cole had accepted Marcus but demanded to know his story.

'The truth, nothing but the truth' He had demanded from him.

Marcus told him the truth and Brother Cole accepted him into the shelter. The shelter was only for homeless men. It was located off Mariankatu Street behind the Korean house. It was an old eight-bedroom building that was renovated and now houses twenty-one inmates from five countries. The inmates have a thirty-minute prayer first thing in the morning and clean up the house before returning to clean their rooms. Everyone goes out afterwards, either to a job or in search of one. The house usually becomes quiet and almost empty throughout the day. One main meal served daily was dinner. Five inmates who work at night are the only occupants around during the day with Marcus and Brother Cole.

Marcus and Brother Cole became close because of their love for music. Bro Cole played the keyboard, guitar and trumpet; he had grown up among African Americans and loved jazz music. He had also fallen in love with a black lady whose father was a missionary. They had gone to Gambia and Senegal together and planned to get married after their missionary studies. In their second year in the missionary college, they went on holiday to South Africa but were attacked by robbers in Soweto. Gale was badly stabbed and died in surgery. After mourning his beloved, Cole committed his life to the missionary work they had both loved. Her picture was at the entrance of the shelter.

One afternoon in the chapel, Marcus played the keyboard while Brother Cole blew the trumpet, Fidan played the guitar and they performed an upbeat version of 'Amazing grace'. After a wonderful rendition, the three shouted and hugged. Fidan rushed out to attend a job interview. Marcus had been working intermittently as a backup for some inmates where undocumented immigrants were used as unskilled labour. The pay was small but it helped to meet some needs. He was saving up to get travel papers to France or Italy. He was now alone with Brother Cole and there was silence. Cole spoke first.

'I think God wants a better calling than football for you.'

Marcus sighed and rubbed his hands together.

'You are good at the keyboard. I feel you have a higher calling. You know what? Stay here and assist me at the shelter. You will be placed on a stipend and we will work out how to send you to a bible college in the States. You can choose to stay there or come back here and take over this place or go back to Nigeria. I don't know what the Master has in stock for you but I know He cares for you.'

He placed one hand on his shoulders. This was not the first time Bro Cole would speak like this to Marcus.

'Stay'.

It echoed like the voice of his grandmother from Oje many years ago. It rang loud in his ears.

Malchus had been indoors for two weeks. At first, it was because of fear more than shame. It felt like a dream but the blood was surely not a dream. His outer garment was stained with his blood. He had kept the stained clothes as a relic of his reality. The man Jesus had rebuked Peter, the fisherman and had touched him on the ear. The blood stopped and his ear was back in place. He had sat stunned as Jesus was taken away by the soldiers and crowd from Annas and Caiaphas, the high priest. He could not go with them again. For him, it was two weeks of shame as he knew that the other servants would mock and laugh at him.

In those two weeks, he stayed awake most nights, wondering if he had not been healed, he would have become one-eared. Could this Jesus truly be the Messiah, son of God, a saviour as he had claimed to be? His mother knew he was going through some heart-wrenching period and had kept quiet, hoping that he would come out better. One day, under the cover of night, he had gone to the place the disciples were hiding after their leader had been crucified and they claimed he had resurrected like Lazarus, that fake one. But he could not get in because everyone had to open their head covering to enter the place and he was afraid he could be identified as a spy of the high priest.

By the third week, the high priest sent some servants to bring him and when he saw him, he held him and praised him for being a dutiful servant. No one mentioned the episode of the ear loss. Rather, the high priest gave him gifts with some money and posted him to be with the chief guard of the high priest.

'He just had powers from Beelzebub. That was what he used. He is not the son of Yahweh. Lies! All of them are liars. He is now deceiving everyone that he has risen again as He promised'. Caiaphas said as he moved around him.

'The soldiers have confirmed that his followers came to steal His body at night. We shall recover it soon.'

Caiaphas tapped him on the shoulder and almost in a whisper, he said.

'Go back to your post'.

And that was what he did. Week after week, the chief guard at the instruction of the high priest, went after the followers of Christ. Malchus was always in the vanguard. He left home and married the chief guard's niece. He also rose to become the new chief guard to the new high priest after Caiaphas. Three years later, a sect rose, different from those who had followed Christ, and they were leading people away from the temple. The new high priest gave orders that their leader should be arrested. Malchus led the band of guards to arrest the members of the new sect. There was a bloody clash and Malchus sustained injuries in the same ear that Jesus healed and also a knife wound close to the heart. He died two days later.

It was the eleventh day of December in the year 2018. Hazy snow was blowing over the city and the Strasbourg Christmas market was agog as usual. The lights of the Christmas decorations were resplendent. Marcus arrived in France two months ago. It was a four-week journey through Sweden, Norway and Germany by land and sea. It had cost him two thousand euros through a network of traffickers and underground immigration collaborators. He had always thought corruption was an African thing but now he knew otherwise.

He arrived in France in the middle of October and had to face the reality of language shock. Finland was a bit better because of their willingness to speak the English language after Finnish and Swedish. Since France was a tourist destination, getting a job as a sole English speaker was not difficult but he learned within a short period, that he needed to acquire the language if he was to get a better job and also fit into a football academy or team. He knew that working to raise money for French classes and other basic needs was of the utmost. No more shelter homes as he was already connected to the African quarters in the city and was sharing a flat.

A customer entered the African shop where he worked, asking for Africa-themed lights for Christmas. He guided the customer around and eventually helped her to make a decision.

'Merci', the customer said as she moved to the entrance with her shopping bag.

'Vous etes les bienvenus' Marcus answered. "You are welcome"; repeating the French words in English. He was used to that.

As he went back to his service agent desk, he remembered his last day in Helsinki. He could not bear to face Brother Cole and say goodbye. His three months with the missionary had almost changed his dream from football to music and mission work.

He had quietly declined to go to a mission college. He planned his exit for when Brother Cole visited hospitals to share food and pray with the sick. The goodbye note was left on the piano that Brother Cole played each night before night prayers.

Dear Brother Cole,

I could not face you to say goodbye. You have been an angel and a beautiful soul. The world needs more people like you. I wish I could be like you but I am not. This dream still burns deep in my bones. I must pursue it. I pray to see you soon one day. Please be rest assured that when my dreams come true, I would come back here to be a blessing more than I have been blessed. Bye for now.

Truly yours,

Marcus.

'My friend, how are you today?'

Khalifa jolted him back to the store with his deep baritone.

'Fine, big man' Marcus answered the broad-shouldered Algerian who was in the haulage section. He had moved in some shipments into the back of the shop and now needed to sign off some papers. Just then, Jackie came in from the staff service area for him to hand over the shift. Jackie was a student from Ghana who was working as a part-time model apart from being a shop attendant. She attended school by day and worked in the shop at night; in between, she was a model.

Marcus worked during the day and attended French classes for four hours at night. As they did the handing over of cash and sales for the day shift, Marcus hurried off to get dinner and get some rest before his ten-minute walk to the night class two streets away.

His dinner was Baguettes, garbure and vegetable salad. He was getting used to French cuisine but always look forward to the weekly African dinner laced with Afrobeat music with Nonso and Kofi on Saturday night at the African kitchen. He paid for the meal and glanced at his watch, it was 19:45. He pulled his bag and strapped it on his back as he walked down the street towards the open arcade.

Five minutes later, he was at the end of the street. He turned and, in a flash, from the side of his eyes, he saw a gun pulled out and bullets sprayed everywhere. He felt a jerk on his chest, then his head. It was a hot searing pain and a loud noise of artillery and screams. The flight of many to safety and the warm flow that wet his hands as he clutched his chest were all he could remember. It was 19:50, on the 11th of December, 2018.

EUNUCH

A new day broke in the king's palace with muffled activities; the court bard sang a ballad in low tones and chanted panegyrics of king Salim. Gondar; the capital city of the Ethiopian kingdom was quiet this morning. Cleaning of the royal palace was still on from the previous day's feast and fight.

King Salim was being attended to by queen Candace and the royal physicians. Omari and Almaya came and bowed to the king in his early seventies, laid on a large chamber bed outside his bedroom. A muffled groan came from the heavily injured ruler. The queen stepped out from the king's caregiving area and moved to the royal courtyard overlooking the city with two loyal senior court officials.

The city was well planned out. The royal quarters were after the king's guard and military quarters. The supreme council members and the members of the king's royal council had their homes outside the military quarters. The city was divided into different quarters, separated by family lineage. Families built houses within their apportioned land while strangers from other kingdoms had their quarters separately, leading to the different markets. The open space used for festivals is bigger than the open space before the royal court, meant for small town meetings. After these open spaces are various markets leading to the four different city gates. This was the layout of Gondar, the main city of the Ethiopian kingdom.

'How is my king today, great queen?' Omari asked as they moved into another room.

'Hmmm. Not too good. He was in pain all through the night. The physicians said that he lost a lot of blood and age is not on his side. They are giving him herbs to help replace lost blood', she explained with a grimace.

The event of the previous day was still like a nightmare to all. The whole city was quiet and calm. Throughout the night; the land had been ravaged and rattled with battles and many arrests had been made of members of the insurrection.

The king's brother, high prince Salana, had shown interest in the throne for his son, claiming that the crown prince who had been dumb since birth could not lead the Ethiopian kingdom. Though he was aware of the crown prince's great improvement, he felt that his son was ready and should be next in line to the throne. A battle ensued when the king got enraged by his brother's comments. The high prince was a retired war general and he had some of his guards around him. They tried getting him to safety and protect him from getting arrested for treason.

Many lives were lost on both sides. The army in the king's palace and some loyal generals were able to squash the insurrection but not before the king was fatally injured. The high prince and most of his men did not make it.

'Have all the royal princes been informed of the king's health?' Almaya asked the queen now.

The queen shook her head; 'Uhmm hmmm, there's no need'.

'High prince Salana has just been buried. Gyesi has left the city with his mother and brothers. It's been rumoured that they are running to Juba or Bangui to hide and wait for the return of General Panya'. Omari informed the queen.

'My queen, the king needs to heal. General Panya and high prince Salana are two of a kind. Panya will push for Gyesi to be put on the throne. With the condition of the king and with the army behind him, the supreme council may bow to his wish. We need to act fast.' Almaya, the head of the treasury, cautioned.

'To do what? My son is not ready and the king needs time,' the queen explained.

'Banish General Panya and Salana's family. Tell the council it was the king's decision. We will support you at the supreme council. Also, get the council to make Omari the new army general so that he can take charge of the army and make them loyal to my king.' Almaya advised.

The side door opens and a senior guard rushes in.

'My queen, my queen… the king…the physicians call for you'. They all rush out.

Omari turns to Almaya, 'Get the scribe to convene the supreme council'. He runs to join the queen.

The king's death was kept a secret until the supreme council convened. The queen was given the sceptre to act as regent until her son was ready to take over the throne. Omari was given full authority over the army, while Salana's family were banned for treason with General Panya as an accessory to the treason charge. The king was buried after seven days of mourning and passage rites.

One month later, Zara was in the garden playing the flute while Almaya came in with a servant, carrying a basket of flowers with drinks and confectioneries. He sat and listened as she acknowledged him without breaking the flow of the rendition.

Almaya started a poetic rendition to accompany Zara's music;

The birds look for a place to stay,

The sun seeks a bed at the cool of the day.

Moon yawns yet is awake for the night,

I am maimed but not slain at heart.

My love seeks a singer, louder than my cry,

One whom my wish could try.

You this could be.

Zara played the flute to the poem as Almaya brought out a gold chain from his pocket and looped it around her neck while humming the tune. She stopped the music and removed the chain to examine it.

'Thank you. It is beautiful', she said almost inaudibly.

'It is nothing compared to you, my beautiful one.'

'But where can this lead us?' Zara asks

'Is there anyone else?' Almaya asked.

'None, but you!'

'Yes, me. Is love about children? Tell me, the man who goes to war and loses an arm or leg, does he stop loving? Love, my love is a thing of the heart. My heart beats and pumps not only blood but love. And my love is not for any other but you since I have set my eyes on you.'

'Where does this lead us? You come from a lineage that is forever loyal to the throne, with riches that cannot be shared with a woman and a family. How would you change that? Treat my heart gently. Let it not enter the ocean and be swept away'.

Zara looked at the full moon on her bed. It seemed the moon was yawning and about to sleep, the cloud covered her eyes just for a moment.

'Take a chance, hope is the wine that keeps the bones alive'. I will go to Jerusalem to seek redemption for my soul, my body and to your ward; the prince. Just maybe, all that we have heard about that great Master can smile a fortune to us too. The queen will give anything to that man or woman who will make her happy and make her son the next king. I hope to bring that happiness and also make our joy come forth.'

Almaya was now holding Zara.

'I wish, I just wish…' She holds his hands to her face. 'But what is the worth of my wish? You are still you. What will come forth from our union?'

'I am a man still. It is only that I can't father a child. Is love just to father children? We can hold what we have dear till old age. You and I can be together forever. '

The sounds of birds chirping and the eerie noise from night animals filled the silence momentarily.

'Please, promise that you will wait for me. Then I will ask the queen, her majesty, to grant me a release from this burden I inherited from my forefathers. Promise that this our love will not end as a dream. Please wait for me and when I come back in six months, I shall ask the queen to bless us after her son is healed.'

Almaya spoke with confidence and vigour but Zara was unsure of what to believe. And when she spoke, she said 'I promise to wait; I just hope this will come out good for us', as she held his hand.

General Panya and Prince Gyesi were in the palace courts waiting to see the king of Juba. General Panya had received news of his exile on his way back from taking a wife from the lower Niger - a princess of Ibadan near the old Oyo kingdom. It was painful that a lot happened behind him and he could do nothing to save his dear friend, the high prince Salana from death and help give him his long-sought dream of the throne.

Omari, that young ambitious man, seized the opportunity to get to his post. Soon, very soon, they will all pay dearly for the betrayal, including Almaya, the eunuch. He was certainly a part of this. Both were too young and ambitious. He controlled the treasury and he had the queen's ears too. The problem now is that no army is loyal to him. Otherwise, he would have taken over the throne and handed it over to Gyesi who was like a son to him.

Prince Gyesi and his mother had met him with a few personal soldiers loyal to the high prince at Juba but they were too few to execute a war that would capture the throne. The king of Juba had been gracious enough to allow them to settle in one of the royal guest houses outside the city.

Now, they want to have an audience with him and make a request months after receiving them in Juba. The trumpet blew as the royal majesty of the Juba kingdom walked into the royal courts. After exchanging pleasantries, the royal bard chanted the panegyrics of the king's heritage. General Panya and Prince Gyesi were introduced to the king of Juba again.

'You may now present your request before His royal majesty, king Asula of Juba kingdom'. The royal bard announced.

General Panya moved forward and took a bow before king Asula.

'Long live His royal Majesty. I come today with high prince Gyesi of the Ethiopians. We come with gratitude for the hospitality your majesty has shown to us; the royal prince's family and my men. May you reign long on the throne of your fathers my lord', Panya spoke as the king shook his royal staff of office at him.

'Home calls my lord. This high prince must go back home to reclaim what rightfully belongs to him. Your people have been good to us but we need to go home and serve our people. We need to foster better ties with great Juba as we have learnt in these few months that Juba has a lot for our great kingdom. Given this my lord, we request the support of your great army to go with us and take back the throne for my prince'.

'I heard that the throne does not belong to your prince here'. The king replied.

'Lies my lord. The throne belongs to Prince Gyesi. The custom of our people allows the brother of the reigning king or his son to take over the throne. High prince Salana had passed the throne to his son, Prince Gyesi before he died. But traitors will see none of this.'

'Hmmm', the king sighs.

'The kingdom of Ethiopia is ruled today by a woman!' General Panya spat out.

'I heard she is a great warrior too.'

'Not before your great army of Juba'

'Ethiopia has a great army and Juba does not fight another man's battle. We fight our battles', the king explained.

'My prince promises your royal majesty vast acres of land in the southern part of the kingdom as a token of our respect to Juba. The land we are offering is rich in gold and spices. Please, help my prince to regain the throne. Our kingdom under my prince shall do well with Juba. We shall never forget your kindness, my lord.'

The king raised his staff as the royal bard announced that the king is about to make a pronouncement that cannot be changed.

'Juba will support Prince Gyesi to get his throne back with ten bands of soldiers if he will get other kingdoms to fight with him. Juba will not fight Ethiopia alone.'

'Long live Juba. My lord has spoken'. The royal trumpet sounded and drums were beaten. All subjects faced down as the King left the court.

'The king invites you to lunch your lordship' the bard announced as he leaves to follow the king's entourage.

'Not bad my prince, a good start that was. We shall get more kingdoms to go with us; the kingdom of your father shall be yours, I promise you.' General Panya tapped Gyesi on the back.

The whole city of Gondar in Ethiopia celebrated the return of Almaya the eunuch; the treasurer of Queen Candace. Almaya is respected in the entire kingdom for his wisdom, humility and compassion for the people. With wisdom, he opened a treasury for people in need and they pay back through taxes which further enrich the kingdom. He had just come back from a pilgrimage to the faraway country of the Jews in Jerusalem. His friend and a notable trader, Naphtali, had invited him to

Jerusalem to observe and celebrate the Passover with him.

Almaya had gone, not only for this feast but also because Naphtali had told him of a man who had turned the land of the Jews upside down. The Master's disciples called him the Messiah, Jesus of Nazareth. Great miracles had been done by the man, Naphtali had said, but he was fiery at driving the traders out of the temple. This was not good for their business and they plotted against him with some religious leaders. Naphtali said they hung the man on a cross but his followers were great like their Master after His death. There were many miracles that Naphtali said His disciples had been performing.

The disciples were taking the message of the gospel everywhere and many nations were accepting the new way. If only this man's followers could help heal the prince. Zara was doing a good job on him and he has greatly improved from being an imbecile to being a strong young man who would command the army one day. He had been taught the customs of the people, the art of war and leadership. But all of this without his speech will not make the prince a great king.

Everyone in the royal council knew that the death of the king had greatly affected the queen, yet she was holding on to her son and would gladly give a fourth of the kingdom to anyone who could make the prince speak to take over the throne. Time was running out as there were rumours about General Panya and Prince Gyesi gathering forces to attack the kingdom. Almaya was hopeful that he would bring a solution from the people of Naphtali. If only the prince could speak, he would ask of the queen, not the fourth of the kingdom, but freedom from this burden that society had laid on his family and lineage.

Now, he was waiting in the garden for Zara. He longed for her beautiful face, her breath, her flute and the songs. He looked at the boxes on the floor containing dresses and gold from the land of the Jews. Zara came in now but her face was cast down. The smiles were gone. Almaya was surprised.

'What happened to you, my love? He quickly asked. His heart ached in an instant.

'The queen said you asked for the prince to be in your custody for some time', she spoke, not looking at his face. She stretched the helm of her robe to straighten it out.

'Yes, my dear…'

She stopped him before he continued.

'She said you brought some powers that will heal the prince and make him whole. Is that true?' Zara asks.

'Yes, my love. It is for the sake of our love. That I may be free to be yours and you mine. I found God, that God that all our gods bow to in the land of Naphtali.' His face glowed as he explained.

'Naphtali took me to his friend's house, a certain tax collector who had met the man who was called the

Christ. Matthew had been one of his followers and was writing the account of the life of the Messiah. I was surprised to find out that he was of the same skin colour as me, though not as dark. There were many like him in Jerusalem. Many of the things Matthew spoke about Jesus were strange and almost unbelievable; the healings, the dead coming to life and many miracles that He did, how His people sold Him to the Romans who crucified Him on the cross.' He stopped for a breath.

'I was disappointed that there was nothing to bring home to heal the prince. Matthew had only given me some scrolls to read of the account of their laws, their prophets and some kings. I left Jerusalem to come home after I had seen many of the places where the account of the Messiah happened.'

'I was reading the book of one prophet Isaiah when suddenly a man came to us from nowhere in the desert to explain many things from the scrolls. Then, some light came to my soul as he spoke and the stories were no longer stories but about life and eternity, about powers beyond our dreams. I knelt in surrender and he prayed with me and baptized me in the water. There and then, my beloved, he was taken away. It was awesome. From then, such love, peace and power filled my soul.'

'So, what now Almaya? What does this have to do with the prince?' She queried.

'After Phillip, for that was his name, left me and my men, joy filled my heart. I touched one of the soldiers who was deaf in one ear and he could hear clearly with both ears. Ajani, my escort, who was blind in one eye began to see with both eyes. The socket empty became filled. It was amazing, we were all dazed. It was like a dream, but it was true.' Almaya spoke, still in awe of his encounter.

'So you came with this your strange power to heal the prince too? After all I have done for him? We are making progress Almaya. I just need more time, more time… and now, you who profess to love me will take away all that I have worked for. Is this what your love is about?' Zara was now distraught.

'Zara, you have tried your best. From the worst situation when the prince could not do anything, you have nursed him into a great warrior, filled with the wisdom of our fathers but he can only talk in signs. The kingdom needs a talking king. Time is no longer on our side. The queen is getting older. The council is more impatient. The people want a king. Panya is gathering an army. We need to act fast. Give me a chance my love. It is for our sake. I wish to ask the queen to set me free that I may be yours, all yours, but the prince must talk first. I know what this power has done to people; let it bring peace to the prince and to us too.' Almaya was now pleading.

'No, Almaya. You may have your way with the queen but …', there was a long silence. She stood and walked to the door. 'Bye, Al. Bye for now.'

Almaya, the eunuch, watched her leave the room. He shook off a tear that wanted to drop from his eyes. He glanced at the chest of boxes filled with robes, dresses and jewellery that he had bought from different kingdoms as he journeyed home to the woman he loved. But now, she was not seeing what he was seeing about their future; his future. This was an opportunity for him to be free from being a eunuch in the courts of the king, with no life outside his service to the king and the kingdom. He wanted to be like other officials of the king, who had wives, and children and were still serving the king in loyalty. Though having children was out of it, for now, he could secure a change for his coming generation.

For two days, Almaya was behind closed doors in his quarters at the expansive palace. He was living only on water and reading from the scrolls for most of the day. He found comfort in the Psalms of David. Zara returned all the boxes of gifts sent to her.

He usually strolled at night in the palace garden with Zara but now that she was gone, he was there this night to gaze at the bright light of the moon and meditate on the Psalms. He was not alone, a hunched-back small figure lurked in the shadows of the rows of the sweet-smelling flowers in the king's garden. It was the royal bard and the king's poet, Zege. He always wore black and would drape a large wrap of the same colour around his body and use the tail end to wrap his white-haired head. He had a gritting voice that sounded like two irons rubbed violently together.

He moved towards him, humming and waving his ubiquitous leopard skin fan. At a distance, he greeted

Almaya who stood to acknowledge the older man. He was very diminutive in size but with a loud gritty voice.

Let her go, let her go

Little flower, blooming bud.

She carries the future king of another clime

Her brew the queens of land not here

Hers are hopes beyond her slight.

Let her go, let her go.

Stolen at the fount of her dreams

Forced to face lands without streams

Captured and sold against her will

Slaved to a beast for a bill.

She is made for another.

Nevermore for you to bother

Let her go, let you go.

Let her go, let her go.

He went out of the garden chanting and waving the fan over his head. Almaya went after him, listening to the chant as if it was the fan that would drive the smoke of her love out of his soul and it did.

Prince Negasi was now ready for Almaya as requested. They were to be together in seclusion where Almaya would read the scrolls to him, especially the songs of David, and entreat the Most High on his behalf. He was hoping that what happened to his men would also happen to Prince Negasi. If they prayed, he would be made whole. At the queen's request, Almaya was led by Omari to the queen who authorised the seclusion with the prince. The days of seclusion began.

The next two months showed some improvement in the prince's condition. Almaya wanted more improvement as the queen was getting impatient. She was getting paler and less visible. There were rumours that she was having a strange disease. She had never been the same beautiful, graceful and motherly queen she was to the king and the kingdom. She was also once a warrior and all of that had gone.

Almaya had visitors from Jerusalem. It was Philip, the one who had been carried away by the wind. He came around with Matthew and Naphtali. They had come with Naphtali who was back to continue his business after the pilgrimage to Jerusalem. Almaya could only go out of the palace quarters with the permission of the queen even though he had a big house outside the palace. Also, Omari and the royal guards have been more tenacious at keeping the prince safe, now that he was showing improvement.

Now that Philip and Matthew were in the kingdom, maybe God will use them to heal the prince. He thought of how to get the visitors to see the prince. It may be hard but there must be a way out. He looked at the scroll he read with Philip and the miraculous healings that happened to his men at the pool after his baptism. He prayed under his breath that their coming will bring about another miracle.

He looked at the prince who was engrossed in reading from the scrolls. His eyes sparked each time he read from the scroll and traced the lines with his fingers. Almaya was always bemused because he knew the prince could not read Aramaic unlike him but used his knowledge of Amharic to decode the letters on the scroll.

The opportunity came a few days later when Omari was asked to represent the queen at the coronation of a village chief. Almaya was able to get Phillip and Matthew into the courts of the prince for a vigil and by daybreak, the miracle happened. The prince's tongue loosened and he could talk, although like that of a baby learning to speak. Almaya's joy knew no bounds. The two disciples were smuggled out again and it was agreed upon that the queen should not be informed of what had happened until she visited the prince. He was to pretend to still be dumb.

♣♣♣♣♣♣♣♣♣♣♣♣♣

Two days later, the trumpet signalling a battle sounded from the guards at the watchtower and Omari got signals that some troops were approaching the city from the south. Some wounded soldiers from the neighbouring villages gave Omari details of a raid that happened over the night. It was also said that General Panya and the royal high prince Gyesi were leading the armies of the Juba kingdom, Oyo kingdom and a Fulani tribe towards the capital city. General Panya, knowing the strength of the Ethiopian army, did not approach the capital city from the north where the most fierce and brave warriors were located.

All the entrances to the city were quickly sealed off, while the queen was taken to the bunker in the palace. Tradition forbids that the king or the queen should be in the same building as the crown prince in an event of war. A council of state meeting was called and all the army generals under Omari were given the war alert to mobilize their men. The armoury was opened and soldiers started receiving additional weapons. Another general; Shango, was stationed with the crown prince Negasi and he was moved out of the palace to the king's stronghold under the rocks, close to the northern border. His new condition was still a secret.

Almaya had known that the throne was the target and the only thing that could avert war was if the crown prince could lead the army as the commander-in-chief. This could ward off the attacking armies and a truce with compromises will be made. He quietly convinced the queen to allow General Shango and the crown prince to accompany General Omari to the meeting with General Panya and the armies.

Five regiments were deployed to guard the five entrances to the city capital while three other regiments were stationed miles outside the capital city to ward off the attacking armies. The three attacking armies stopped at the sight of the Ethiopian army to lay a siege on the capital city. They sent emissaries to Omari who led an elite unit to inquire about the purpose of the onslaught. General Panya led the generals of the three kingdoms in asking for the throne of the kingdom for Prince Gyesi since the crown prince was not capable of leading the kingdom. They requested the throne be submitted or it would be taken by brutal force.

Omari and the leaders who attended the meeting on a free battle zone merely laughed and requested to deliver the message to the queen.

After the meeting with the Ethiopian generals, General Panya called an urgent meeting of the three commanders of the attacking armies with the royal High Prince Gyesi. It was a meeting for a change of strategy. He outlined his observation and what a quick change of strategy would achieve.

'Something is wrong somewhere. General Shango and Omari should never have come to that meeting together. While they were here, the queen and the crown prince were not fully covered. As they go back, the supreme council has to be briefed on this meeting and a final decision for war or truce will have to be made. It is a good time to strike', General Panya explained.

'That is just taking a chance,' Ogun from Oyo kingdom cautioned.

'It could be a trap too,' Bello, the Fulani said supporting Ogun.

'I am sure we can catch them unawares now. They are going to meet and use the time in between to bring all the armies from the east and west closer. If we take the queen and the crown prince captive, we will have the kingdom before dawn,' General Panya said with assurance.

The generals of the supporting armies did not agree to take the risk. General Panya and Prince Gyesi led two bands of guerrilla warriors into the city through underground water channels that leads to the palace and the hideout of the crown prince. While the supreme council meeting was going on, General Panya, Prince Gyesi and the warriors entered. The queen was ferried to the inner courts quickly while the battle raged on between Omari, General Shango's men and the invading armies.

Crown prince Negasi led a party to surprise his mother with the cheering news of his miraculous healing at the hands of two strangers who claim to be the friends of Almaya; the eunuch. This was when high prince Gyesi led the warriors to attack his safe house. The two princes were locked in battle as Almaya and the royal guards engaged the guerrilla army. The guerrilla band lost power and was captured but Prince Gyesi was killed. The two army generals; Omari and Shango overpowered General Panya and killed him in the process.

The heads of Panya and Gyesi were sent on a stake that same night to the waiting generals. News of the crown prince's healing spread like wildfire after victory over the invading armies. It was a double celebration for the people. The supreme council requested that he should be crowned immediately and the king's messenger spread the news all over the city. The royal ceremony is to come up later. He was crowned the next morning on the rooftop of the palace, overlooking the city and for the first time in his life, he addressed the people who were still reeling in victory. His speech was short.

The marauding armies sent a message for a truce. They requested not to be attacked on their way home. The new king assured them of safety as he made his first official pronouncement. The queen was happy and requested a private meeting with Almaya and the new king, a few days before the royal celebration and public presentation of the king to the kingdom of Ethiopia.

'Today is the happiest day of my life Almaya. That my son will ascend the throne of his father after years of pain and toil, hope and doubts. I salute your courage Almaya.' The queen glowed with joy. She had become beautiful once again although her brows were lined with tiredness.

'Ask anything you want from us up till a fourth of the kingdom Alamaya and it will be yours. In addition to whatever you ask, we have agreed to give you the third highest title in the land,' king Negasi spoke with a newfound grace and authority.

Going down on one knee before the king and queen mother, Almaya, the eunuch and treasurer of the kingdom with much joy and confidence spoke;

'May you live long my king and queen mother. I request only two things; a land to build a place of worship for my newfound faith. Also, that you graciously grant that no man be made a eunuch before he can serve the throne; so that my clan can be made free to have wives like all the servants of my king and queen mother.'

The king signals for his staff as he hands over the sceptre. He rises to his feet and stamps the staff on the floor three times and ends it with;

'Granted! This becomes law in all the kingdoms of the Ethiopians. Let the royal scribe record this. No man shall be a eunuch again in the land of the Ethiopians and the forest outside of the city before the river is given to Almaya to build a house for his God'. After a long drag by the king whose speech was getting better by the day, the king's bard shouted this in repetition. The drums rolled in royal consent and praise of the king.

That evening, Almaya went home, took a long bath and hurried to Zara's quarters, whom he had not seen in weeks. He went with gifts and with the hope of a new beginning. He was shocked to find her place deserted and clean. He was told she had just left and would be outside the city gate. Almaya rode his horse frantically, leaving his guards behind. He caught up with her, with the company sent by the queen to lead her back home to the kingdom's northern region.

Almaya took her to a sideway, a clearing that was not too far from their two companies. It was a small clearing used by travellers.

'Why did you leave Zara? I am free now; all yours. The new king has granted me the freedom to take a wife and all my clan are free from the age-long bondage. We have made it. Don't go, come back with me Zara. Let us start a new life together.'

'Al, I am happy for you. You are free but things have changed.'

'What has changed? Who has changed?' He asked.

'All of us. You...I. You have found a new love; your faith. I see the glow in your eyes. I know the joy of your soul. I can't compete with that. I must go back to my people. I must seek a new soul to free, lift and build in the way of our fathers, in the wisdom of our forebearers. '

'No Zara, you can come with me. You can discover this new way, truth and life with me ....' he muttered.

His wish for Zara was blowing away like the wind on a hazy day. His heart tore into pieces. He held himself together, a warrior does not weep before his army. He reached out for her hand.

'Please stay a little more. Let us give this one more chance.'

'Bye Al, goodbye Almaya. You are a good man; may you find peace and joy.' She rose and walked back to her company.

She climbed her horse with the help of a servant and rode away in tears. The words of the old sage who she had gone to for counsel the previous day rang in her ears…

'My daughter, the ways of the gods are too deep to understand and the supreme one, too deep to fathom. When you came with a new way to care for and train our prince, the gods bid us listen to you and follow your lead and we did. Did we not know more than you? But it pleases the gods to act in the way they want. Follow your heart and go to the man who loves and wants you.'

Now, she did not look back. She rode away with her head held straight.

Almaya was transfixed for some time and watched as she rode off into the night with her train and the light from their lamps fade. Each horse hoof stamped on the floor was like a stab to his heart and the wheels of the chariots felt like his soul is being dragged on the floor. The light got smaller until it became a dot that soon disappeared. Almaya groaned and growled.

Tears flowed down his face; his love for Zara was as strong as death. His heart ached and burned. He no longer cared if the men around him heard a warrior's cry. Two came to his rescue and helped him onto the horse as they rode back to the city.

He was indoors for days, nursing his pain and loss. He emerged consoled and comforted by his friends.

The vast land given to him outside the city gates became an obsession as he built a place of worship for his newfound faith and Master. His new love for his saviour and master, Jesus was greater than what any man could give him; this propelled him to greater service. Almaya was later recognised as the founder of the first Ethiopian church.

ABOUT THE AUTHOR

Oluwatoyin James Omitogun holds a Bachelors of Arts degree in English Language and Literature. He also has two master's degree in English Literature and Business Administration. He had over two decades career in the banking industry which saw him to a senior management position. Presently, he is self-employed in Agribusiness, Construction and Fashion industries. He Pastors a congregation in Ibadan. A motivational speaker; he has written four books in the last twenty-three years. Monopoly of Grief is his fifth book. He is also an actor, director and producer of Christian drama and film. Married to Omowunmi Adenike and with their Children; they make their home in Ibadan, Oyo state, Nigeria.

Other Books by the Author:

Butterfly's Cocoon, And Other Stories	*– 1999*
The Missing Passport	*- 2006*
Not Just a King	*- 2006*
Why? And Other Stories	*- 2012*

www.ingramcontent.com/pod-product-compliance
Lightning Source LLC
LaVergne TN
LVHW050548160826
845677LV00011B/2225